Table of Contents

Courting Death

Lucia sat in the corner of the hospital room waiting for her patron to die. Somehow, he held on. His life slipped away, but at what seemed to be the last moment, a relative would visit. Idle chatter with his beloved aunt; a gentle hug with his usually crass nephew; an old friend whose bond was closer than blood.

She watched and waited, unseen. His visitors were free with their emotions, and she soaked in the tenderness of this man. At first, she thought it was the love given to him that kept him going, but after a time she realized it was his willingness to give his love that gave him strength.

She'd guided so many into the afterlife; she'd lost count. Nearly a century of walking with the dead had blurred together so thoroughly that she could barely remember them as people, and they had such a nasty habit of fading from her memory. Her patrons had become more a feeling, a soft sadness that melded with her over the years.

The emotions of the recently dead varied widely. The ones who weren't ready crashed into fear and anger. This poisonous blend of resentment and grief had to be quelled before they could proceed; no easy task. Some clung greedily to life as their imagined futures disappeared beneath them. Others were overcome with worry as they left their loved ones to fend for themselves. It was a rare few who embraced the afterlife with joy and excitement.

This man—his name was Oliver--would surely go into the next world full of love and contentment. Never had she seen such a voluminous parade of well-wishers and heartfelt goodbyes. How one person could be so loved was astounding, especially one so young.

But this was not a typical farewell. Families and friends of the dying tended to visit their loved ones to comfort them in their last days, but here, it was reversed. They visited Oliver so he could assuage their fears and offer them solace, which he did so willingly and gracefully.

His father was inconsolable.

"The doctor says another round of chemo could make a difference."

"You know it won't, though." It could have sounded callous, but from Oliver, it was simple truth.

In these moments, Lucia felt she was intruding. This was a final goodbye between a father and son; it was none of her business.

But of course, it was precisely her business.

For a while, they said nothing. They sat in silence, both lost in their individual trains of thought. It had been like this for days. Oliver's father just couldn't let go, but Oliver was intent on waiting patiently.

They were so much alike emotionally and physically. She couldn't help but see the resemblance. The old man was built like a truck, clearly a former athlete, even with his gray hair and wire-rimmed glasses.

3

Although his simple sweater and slacks couldn't hide his bulky frame, his size made him no less gentle, though. Only someone with true compassion could have raised Oliver.

In another life, Oliver could have been a football player or a wrestler like his dad, but he'd been cursed with a cancer that had plagued him from boyhood. Oliver was waifish. He had a head of patchy, short hair that sprouted after he'd chosen to end his treatments. His smile, however, had never wavered. He greeted everyone with genuine happiness, even when they were too grief-stricken to reciprocate.

"You should rest," his father said. Lucia could see his urgent need to slip out of the room and weep alone as men tended to do. For those unaccustomed to powerful bouts of emotion, these moments were often overwhelming. Oliver wouldn't have it, though. If his father needed to weep, he would be there for him.

"Take your time, Dad. I'm not going anywhere."

He held his father's hand as the bull of a man let it out. It came all at once. With the dam punctured, he could not hold back the flood. He wiped tears from his eyes with forearms that could crack steel. Oliver simply held his hand and let his father grieve. Sometimes people must mourn before the actual death.

His father cried a while longer. Eventually, when he'd composed himself, they fell into idle conversation about sports and science and politics. Oliver inquired about who his father was seeing--Lucia had guided Oliver's mother into the afterlife when he was just a boy--but the old man had dedicated himself so completely to his son's recovery that romance had always been a distant concern.

When the conversation reached a lull, Oliver turned to a more serious topic. "Did you bring the suit?"

"I did," his father replied with a hint of reluctance.

"Can I see it?"

"Don't you think this is a bit morbid?"

"I want to see the suit I'll be buried in."

His father sighed and moved to the closet by the doorway. He removed a zipped suit bag.

"You know, I bought this for your graduation."

"I know."

"Shame you never got to wear it."

The words *I will* hung between them. Oliver could have said them, and it would have been true, but also a tad cruel.

His father opened the bag and draped a fitted gray suit with a crisp silver tie over the back of his chair. It came with a black vest and a matching pocket square.

Lucia could tell by Oliver's smile that he loved it. "It's perfect."

His father sat with him until Oliver slipped into sleep. He read for a while until he, too, drifted off.

Their bond was genuine and true, and it gave Oliver strength. The essence that held him to life had grown as his father came to terms with the inevitable. Oliver would survive another night.

Lucia approached the bed, hovering inches off the ground. The moonlight caught her eye and she lifted her veil to get a better look. It was full that night. She breathed in slowly, taking in the moment.

Oliver slept soundly beneath her. At times, his breathing was harsh and ragged, but in this moment, he was at peace. She removed her black glove and held her hand an inch above his forehead. She could end his suffering with a graze, but she hesitated. Was he truly in pain?

Physically, yes, of course. The cancer had pummeled him to the point that he could barely stand. He was fed through a tube and washed by nurses. He was a twenty-four-year-old man in a hospice home that was generally reserved for people who had lived much longer lives. His organs were failing, and though he did his best to hide it while his relatives sat with him, he was in agony.

But it didn't seem to bother him. He'd lived his whole life in the hold of sickness, and he'd long since made his peace with the world. If he'd grown up a peevish, resentful man who felt robbed by life, no one would have blamed him.

Instead, he embraced life to the fullest, at least as much as feeble body allowed. He learned the guitar, piano, and bass. He studied French and Italian, although he never got to visit. He went to culinary school and though he wasn't able to graduate, he was a promising baker.

But most importantly, he cultivated the bonds with his family and friends. Oliver knew from a young age that he wasn't destined for a long life, so he never wasted a moment on petty grudges or ugly words. So to say he was in pain only was partially true.

Would it be a mercy to hasten his demise? Certainly not to his family. There were others like his father who needed a bit more time with him to soak up his resolve and contentment.

She pulled back and decided against it. "Sleep another night. Brighten this world another day."

She reached into the dark folds of her clutch and removed her trusty timepiece. It was stuck on the year 1937, but the gears still ticked, and time passed by with her at its edges.

"Nearly midnight. I'm afraid I must be off. Appointments to keep. I'm sure you'll understand." She slipped her glove back on and brushed Oliver's cheek with the back of her hand.

※ ※ ※

She sat at the bus stop under the glow of the moonlight. She wore her hat low, casting her veil over her pale face. Next to her stood a woman chatting idly on her phone. It was almost her time, but until she passed, she would not see Lucia. Soon enough, though.

Lucia sighed under her veil. "She doesn't even see it coming."

"It's been a rough day," she said into her phone. The woman-- Maria was her name; Lucia knew this as with all her patrons--wore all black. All black on her last day seemed terribly appropriate, but of course, she had no idea.

She wore an apron over a black tie and black slacks. Her hair was neatly pulled back into a bun, but the day had worn away her efforts. It was a frizzy mess. There were stains on the apron from the meals she'd served, and her exhausted expression slowly receded as the person on the other end of the line consoled her.

"I'm almost home. I can't wait to see you."

The light turned green and Maria made her way across the intersection, more concerned with her conversation than the road. Too many died this way, seeking a bit of solace in whatever refuge suited them.

The driver tried to stop, but he was going too fast. Maria flew from the impact, her phone shattering before she did. The headlights of the pickup highlighted her in her last moment.

"My name's Lucia."

The ghostly apparition rose from within Maria, and Lucia held her hand, lifting her up off the pavement.

They usually didn't want to admit it, but they knew immediately. It wasn't a question of seeing or being told; it was an innate knowledge. The human spirit knew how to respond to death, just as the human body knew how to respond to birth.

"Is that it?" This new Maria stood over her former self, holding her hand to her mouth as if it would quell the gasping of her breath.

"I'm afraid so." Lucia stood at her side, ready to offer whatever comfort or guidance Maria might need. She preferred to let them take a few moments to absorb the reality of the situation and gauge their reaction.

The driver stumbled out of his truck in a panic. He was dripping with sweat and on the verge of hyperventilating.

"Oh god...lady? Are you okay?" He knelt next to Maria and reached down to feel her pulse, but before he touched her skin, he recoiled. "Holy shit..."

He glanced at his truck. The only damage was a nasty dent in the thick chrome grill.

"I'm sorry," he said to the dead woman as he scurried to make his getaway.

Maria chased him as he peeled off. "You can't just leave me here." When she stopped running, she found herself looking down over the cracked shell of her phone. "Someone has to tell Sofia."

"It'll be all right." Lucia hovered nearby, shrouded in the fog that forever trailed her.

"It's not all right," Maria snapped. "That asshole left me to rot in the street."

"That's not you anymore. It's time to leave it behind."

Maria turned to face Lucia. It was as if she'd just noticed her for the first time. The look of fear and revulsion was familiar to Lucia, but no less painful.

"What are you, some kind of demon come to drag me off to hell?"

The veil hid Lucia's face and Maria could not see her wince, as if her words were physical blows. "I'm no such thing," Lucia said a bit more icily than she'd intended. She took a breath and let the venom leave her voice. "I am your guide. I don't know what awaits you, but I will see you safely to your destination."

"Like hell you will, witch." Maria took off running. She made it to the end of the block and turned the corner, only to find Lucia blocking her path, calmly holding her clutch.

"It's time."

She ran again. Her ghostly transparency seemed to make her disappear each time she stepped into the shadow, only to reappear under each street lamp. Lucia sighed at the futility of it all, and with a thought, she was in front of Maria again.

"It's your time, Maria."

She pounded her fists on her knees and screamed. "Sofia's waiting for me!" Her screams turned to sobs. "She doesn't even know I'm gone."

"She will. She'll miss you dearly and she'll mourn, and in time, she'll move on. In one sense you'll be gone, but you'll always be with her. Such is death." Lucia extended her gloved hand, but Maria hesitated. "These are no longer your concerns."

After some time, Maria took Lucia's hand and they walked together down the quiet street. The streetlamps hemmed the light and shadow, and they dipped in and out of the glow until Maria was gone and Lucia walked alone.

She walked by herself for a time, trying to keep the memory of Maria a bit longer. Her patrons slipped away so fast, no matter how hard she fought to keep them. The souls of the dead drifted off like half-remembered dreams, and she was left with nothing but a feeling. There was always sorrow, but this one--*what was her name?*--had left her with shame and anger.

They never intended to, but people were hurtful. For many, it was a moment of profound fear and loss, so she tried her best not to hold it against them. Still, they wounded her.

She followed the path of the streetlamps. A few steps in the light, a few in the dark. She hadn't realized she was lonely until she had company. As she stepped from the shadow, she noticed her sister walking beside her.

"Hello, Esmerelda."

"Little Lucia. How was your evening?"

"Exhausting."

Esmerelda took Lucia's hand and they walked in silence as they had so often before. How Lucia would have survived these long years without her stalwart sister, she could not begin to imagine.

Esmerelda's confidence gave Lucia strength and her humor lightened Lucia's dour moods. She was so sure of herself, and everything about her reflected that simple truth.

Esmerelda, like Lucia, would forever wear what she had been wearing at the moment the zeppelin hit the ground. Her dress had been a chic lavender crusted with rhinestone chevrons. Death had faded it to black, yet she still had an air of leisure and sophistication. She donned silk stockings and stilettos and a cloche hat with a white rose, all turned black. Esmerelda always dressed to impress; she could have died any day and she would have spent eternity in elegance.

Lucia, on the other hand, was fate's whipping girl, destined to spend her afterlife dressed like a widow in mourning. When Lucia died, she'd been wearing a prim white dress, satin gloves, and a wide-brimmed hat with a veil. She thought she'd dressed for a summer garden soiree, but fate had deigned to take her life along with her colors. Black was appropriate for her role, but only left her maudlin.

They stepped through the familiar gates of their resting place, the Cemetery Poblenou. It was well past midnight, so aside from the droning of a few wandering spirits, the old stones were silent.

They made their way past the famous sculpture of death in a lover's embrace; that handsome young man, limp in the arms of a winged skeleton, resigned to a final kiss.

Lucia hated that statue. This is what people thought of her. She was a monster to be feared; a winged beast descending upon them to steal their mortal breath. How she loathed the depiction. She loathed the fear it invoked. She loathed the way it fetishized the moment of death, as if there was something romantic in it.

But most of all, she loathed the sick pleasure that the bringer of death seemed to take in the act, as if it were a joy to see a life end. She'd learned long ago that the dead could not be spared their fate, nor should they be. Death served a purpose. Her work was important, and at times she even took pride in it, but there was no joy in it. None at all.

They walked through the corridors of raised mausoleums. They knew where their bodies lay, but often they took circuitous routes just to enjoy the few moments they had to walk together.

When finally they arrived at their graves, they sat on a nearby bench and stared up at the moon. They were in the long rows of wall vault crypts where the tombs were stacked on top of one another. Wreaths of flowers were clipped to the newer headstones, but Lucia's and Esmerelda's visitors had long since passed on.

Lucia stared at her tomb. *Lucia Negrín, 1912-1937.* It didn't bother her that she had died young, although, it had for a long time. What bothered her was that she wasn't given the same path into the next world as those she guided.

She and her sister, who had only lived seven years longer, were thrust into their role by fate without a chance to argue their case. It might not have been so hard to bear if their patrons could just appreciate what they did for them. People were often as cruel as fate.

"Why do they hate us?"

"Not this again, Luci." Esmerelda rolled her eyes. "We bring death. You remember how you felt at our time."

"We don't bring death. We offer guidance."

"So you say, dear sister."

Lucia rested her chin in her palm and let out a huff. "I may have been scared at our time, but Charles was there to teach us. He showed us the way. Without him, where would we be?"

"Charles was a ponce."

"Esmerelda!" Lucia gave her sister a light slap on the wrist. "Charles was happy to have our company. It was an honor to see him into the next world."

"He'd have been happier if we were strapping young sailors." Esmerelda grinned wickedly and laughed at her own joke. Lucia, however, did not find it funny. She crossed her arms and turned away from Esmerelda. "Oh, come on, Luci. Live a little!"

"Is that supposed to be funny?"

"I'm laughing."

Esmerelda scooted across the bench and nestled her head on Lucia's shoulder. For a while, Lucia coldly ignored her, but she could only stay angry with her sister for so long. She took Esmerelda's hand.

"I just want to help them."

"They're not scared of *you*, Luci. You must see the distinction."

"I wish that were true."

The tears rolled out of Lucia's eyes without her permission. She hated crying in front of Esmerelda. Whenever she was overcome with melancholy, she turned to her sister. What a burden. Esmerelda, for her part, was always quick to oblige.

"Sweet little Lucia, your heart always was too big for this world." Esmerelda wiped the tears from Lucia's cheek with her kerchief. "But I suppose it's that big heart of yours that makes you so fit for this line of work."

✳ ✳ ✳

Lucia stood over Oliver's bed in the dark hours of the night. At some point in the evening, his father had left, presumably to sleep in a proper bed, or maybe because there was a limit to how long he could watch his son wither. Oliver looked so peaceful, illuminated only by the light of the moon and the glow of the machines that kept him breathing. She'd waited long enough. It was his time.

"You're back," he said. His eyes fluttered, and a weak smile stretched across his face.

Lucia was taken aback. "You can see me?"

"The whole time. I appreciate you watching over me. I was wondering when you'd say hello."

"Oh no. This isn't good. No no no. You're not supposed to be able to see me. You don't deserve this." She felt a heat rise in her cheeks--though surely it was a phantom feeling as hot and cold had faded away long ago--and she fanned herself with her hand.

Oliver, however, remained calm. "What's the matter?"

He reached out for her hand, but she recoiled. "You can't. Maybe you should have some more time. Is there anyone else you need to say goodbye to?" She paced. If she'd still had a heartbeat, it would have been racing.

"What's your name?"

"This is how it was with Charles. Esmerelda and I saw him in the lounge. He was alone and he wouldn't stop staring at us. He wasn't the only one there, but he was ours."

"Miss." Oliver coughed, at first trying to get her attention, but then violently as his chest seized. She rushed to his side and knelt beside the bed. When his coughing fit subsided, he asked, "What's your name?"

"Lucia."

"I'm Oliver."

He held his hand out for a cordial shake, but she shook her head. "You're not ready for that."

Despite her fear and anxiety, he still smiled at her. He wasn't the least bit shaken by her. In fact, he seemed concerned for her.

"Tell me what's wrong. You seem upset."

She took a deep breath to compose herself. "Your time in this world is almost up."

He laughed. "That much I know."

"But you haven't passed yet, and the fact that you can see me means..." The words stuck in her throat and she could not bring herself to tell him.

He took her hand in his, and this time she wasn't quick enough in pulling away. Fortunately, she had her gloves on. "Go on."

She took a deep breath and let the words spill out. "It means that when you die, you'll end up...like me."

"And what could be so wrong with that?"

"You're not scared? Most people think I'm a monster."

"Are you?"

"No."

"Then there's nothing to be scared of."

She laughed at the beautiful simplicity of his logic.

"It's not an easy job."

"Nothing worth doing ever is." He mustered all the strength left within him and pushed himself upright. "I'm ready. I have been for a long time."

Lucia took a quick glance at him. She shook her head and smiled. "This won't do."

"What?"

"A hospital gown. We can't welcome you to eternity dressed like that." She looked over her shoulder and saw the suit where his father had left it, draped over the back of the chair. "I think you should change."

"I'll need your help."

She flinched at the thought of touching him, even though they'd already held hands. Touch was something she'd grown to mistrust, but he needed her help, and so he would have it.

She held him under his arms and lifted him out of the bed, being careful not to let him touch her skin. She held him up and helped him balance.

"You're strong."

She giggled. "Well there are certain advantages." She unzipped the suit bag and removed a white button-up shirt and the charcoal gray jacket. "This will be black once you've crossed over. All of it will."

"Black is slimming," he said with a chuckle.

He meant it as a joke, but it was unnerving how gaunt he was. Death would fill him out, so at least that was a consolation. The ones who died from sickness seemed to find some solace in having their bodies restored.

She handed him the shirt and turned away. "It isn't appropriate for me to look."

"Stay close. I'll need to hold on to you."

It took quite a long time, but eventually he put on his shirt and pants. He held her shoulder when his legs grew unsteady. She helped him slip on his shoes and socks and guided his arms into the jacket. She offered to help him with his tie, though she had no idea how to tie it. Luckily, he was able to do that much on his own.

"How do I look?"

The suit was far too big. It might have fit him at some point, but now it hung off him like a bathrobe.

"Are you ready?" She held his hands and gave him a meek smile, trying to give him courage, but it was she who needed to muster her nerve.

"Yes. How do we do this?"

"A touch will suffice."

"How about a kiss?" Surely if she still had blood in her veins, she would have blushed. "Like the statue at Poblenou Cemetery."

"I hate that thing."

"I think it's romantic. What's so bad about it?"

All the things she hated about the sculpture rushed to the tip of her tongue, only to get tangled and jumbled until she couldn't say anything other than, "It just is."

Oliver didn't press the issue. "I understand. A touch, then."

"No." She realized how much she wanted a kiss. It hadn't entered her mind before he'd suggested it, but suddenly it was all she wanted. "A kiss."

She closed her eyes and leaned in close. He lifted her veil and said, "You're beautiful."

She was just about to kiss him, but she pulled away at the last moment. "Wait. One last thing." She removed her gloves and handed them to him. "You'll be glad to have them." They were snug on him, but she assured him. "Death has a way of sorting things out." With that, he pulled her close.

She pressed her lips to his and felt the familiar tingle of a life slipping away. It was so common, yet this time so exhilarating. The thought crossed her mind that she hadn't kissed anyone in over eighty years.

His body slumped down as his soul separated. He stood before her in his new form...or, in another sense, his old form. Oliver was a thick man like his father. The suit had filled out and she saw how handsome he had once been in life with a thick beard and his hair parted into a neat coif.

He stepped to the side of his former self and looked down at it. "I won't miss that body."

"You're so confident. When I passed, I was a screaming wreak."

"I had a lot of time to come to terms with it."

A strange sensation came over Lucia, like an effervescence bubbling up from her toes that threatened to lift off the ground.

"This can't be. Not now."

"What?"

"I think I'm moving on." She took him in her arms and squeezed tight. "I didn't know I wanted this, and now I can't have it. Why is fate so cruel?"

"It's your time. Maybe you've fulfilled your purpose. You guided so many, and now you've guided me into this new role."

She laughed through the tears. "Guided you, what a joke. It was the other way around."

She kissed him again and held her lips to his until she was gone.

Oliver stood over his body, contemplating what would come next. He didn't have a clue, but a whole new life--for lack of a better term--awaited him. He would miss Lucia, but he was glad to have helped her move on.

"That was a good thing you did."

Oliver turned and saw an elegantly dressed woman standing in the doorway. She looked like she'd stepped out of a smoky jazz club.

"It was the least I could do for her."

"I think you'll be pretty good at this." She headed off down the hall, waving for him to follow. "Come on, then. I'll show you the ropes."

Killing Time

It's 1:00am. Slow. On a Wednesday. Or is it Thursday? It's slow. Nothing happening. It's February or April or May, June, July...all the same. It's 1:00am, and it's slow.

Zach is trying to read. Reading passes the time. Minutes disappear in large chunks behind the pages of a book. It's easy to get lost in a book. It's a good way to kill time. He's reading *1984*, but he hasn't read very much.

It was a bright-

The phone rings. He lets it ring. Once. Twice. Three times. He stares at it, but it's only a plastic blur and a flashing red light. Zach is nearsighted. He can see the words on his page clearly, but the phone is only a few feet away and it's a blur. He studies the cover of his book instead, staring into the wide blue eye of Big Brother looking back at him. All the while, the phone keeps ringing. He's hoping it'll stop. Maybe if he can't see it clearly, it'll stop. It doesn't.

He repeats a script he's internalized. "Empire Hotel, how can I help you? Towels. Four towels. There's no bellman at 1:00am. No bellman past midnight." He asks politely, "Would you mind stopping at the front desk, because, you see, there's no bellman at this hour, sir?" But, as usual, the answer is no.

Grumbling. Moaning. Whining. That's all these people do. Everything is too hard for them. A king suite a block off Michigan Avenue, complimentary Wi-Fi, a bath and a half. Not enough. He's out of his chair and upstairs with four towels. He doesn't bother to bring his glasses. Elevator up. He leans in close to read the buttons. Tenth floor. Knock knock. *Leave the towels at the door,* the portly blur says. Yes sir. Back to the elevator. Thanks for the tip, asshole.

There's a line at the front desk. Men in tuxedos. Women in silk and satin. "Hey, is there a liquor store around here?" a voice asks. "We're with the wedding party," the voice says. Zach is walking down the hall from the elevator bank. He can't tell who spoke to him. He approaches the group, getting close enough to see there are ten or so. They all have tattoos and they all have beers. He can smell it. There are a few people waiting at the front desk. The others are standing by the entrance, leaning against the door of the Supper Club.

Zach moves past the women at the foyer, around the couches where there are a few couples sipping Heinekens, past the men leaning on the front desk, and through the employees-only door back to his post. He doesn't know who asked about the liquor store, but there's a man leaning over the desk with beer on his breath and a tie around his head, so he addresses this man. "Michigan and Chicago. There's a Walgreens. It's twenty-four hours." Whether or not they sell liquor, Zach isn't sure, but it's the only bet at 1:00am.

They chug their beers, leave the cans for Zach to throw away, gather a few of the women idling by the Supper Club, and head out in search of more beer. A gust of wind enters as they exit. Under the desk, just below the monitor is a row of knobs and switches. Zach turns a knob, the lights swell, the marble top of the desk shimmers, and he's back to his book.

It was a bright, cold day in April, and the clocks were striking thirteen-

"Hi. I'm Tina."

He doesn't bother to stand up or even put on his jacket. Without his glasses he can only see the words on the page, but he doesn't bother to put them on. He still has one finger in the book, even though he's still on the first line.

There's a hand holding a glass extended in his direction, and it's covered in tattoos. The whole arm is inked, but he can't distinguish one image from another. There's a face. A smiling face with black hair. He's squinting, but he can't make out the details without his glasses.

"How can I help you? Is there something you need?"

"I've got everything I need right here." She rests her drink on the front desk. Whiskey on the rocks. He can smell it. "Do you? How 'bout a drink?"

"I can't drink. I'm working. I'd get fired." Zach is the only one there besides the valet, and he wouldn't say anything. Zach could drink if he wanted to. Of course, there's the matter of the cameras. The lobby is full of cameras, supposedly looking down on the guests, but really, it's Zach they're interested in. The ones pulling the strings, the big shots at the Empire Hotel can tap into the feed whenever they like, from their homes! They could tune in at any moment, and god forbid, Zach get caught with a Rum and Coke, a flute of champagne, a shot of tequila...

It's a tough economy out there. Jobs with medical and dental don't grow on trees. He can't risk his eight hours a day, five days a week, fifty-two weeks a year. Zach has bills. Gas, electric, Wi-Fi, phone. He has student loans to pay off. Thirteen dollars an hour. Eight hours to read *1984.* 11:00pm to 7:00am.

"One drink," she says, squinting at his name tag. "Zachary Winston. One drink won't hurt."

"I'll lose my job. No, thank you." He's staring longingly at his book, hoping she'll leave if he just plays along.

"Come on, *Zachary.* What are you, twenty-three? Twenty-four?"

"Twenty-nine."

"You're still young. Live a little!"

"No, thank you." He closes *1984* and pushes it aside. "Is there something I can help you with?"

"Great book you have there, by the way," she says. She's trying to reach over the counter and grab it, but she's not tall enough. "If it weren't for that book, I might not have stopped. Bald head, moderately handsome. I bet those look good on you," she says, eyeing his thick, black-rimmed glasses resting next to the book. "I might have stopped, but the book was a game changer. I have a soft spot for the classics."

She's forward and direct. Zach can't tell if it's the alcohol or just her nature. He can't rid himself of her without a conversation, and someone so demanding deserves at least the courtesy of being seen. He puts on his glasses and is amazed by the beauty of the woman in front of him.

"How do I look?" Her arms are up in the air and she's spinning in slow circles.

"Wow," Zach says under his breath.

There's a black dress and blond highlights and black mascara, but where to start? Good lord, where to start? There are black high heels and black stockings. There's an eyebrow piercing; earrings, nearly a half dozen; and hair that flows around her shoulders. There's a b-cup bra edging out ever so slightly from beneath the dress, and short sleeves that don't go past the triceps. And blue eyes, strange blue eyes. *Colored contacts,* Zach thinks, but it doesn't matter. The blue is enchanting.

And of course, there are tattoos. Dozens. No, hundreds. No, thousands. They are hard to count. Her arms are collages. Her chest is a mural. There's more ink under her stockings. The skin of her face is all that's unmarked. Even her neck is inked. There are spades, clubs, hearts, and diamonds wrapped around her wrists. Dragons clawing at her forearms. Spider webs curled around her elbows. Nautical stars, demons, pin-up girls, fireballs, pills, knives, guns, flames, faces, ghosts, ships,

26

words, sentences, spears, gas masks, skeletons, tree stumps, bricks, hawks, a goldfish, and a pair of pliers. And that's just at first glance.

"How about that drink, Mr. Winston?" But before he can reply, she's off, headed out into the cold without a jacket. He tries to read his book, and even though he's alone, and even though the phone isn't ringing, he can't distinguish the words. He's so enamored that he forgot to take off his glasses. The words are nothing but blobs of ink. His vision has shifted.

She's standing outside the foyer by the valet's podium with a few members of the wedding party, huddled together under the valet's heat lamps. They're all smoking cigarettes. At this point, he gives up any pretense of reading and pushes the book aside. He stares at her, admires her.

He could fit in with that group. There are three men and two women, and they all look like Tina. The men are tall with slicked back hair. They have tattoos and piercings. They don't look the type to wear suits, but they wear them well. Both women wear small black fedoras with pinstripes and silk sashes around the brims, as if they'd coordinated the ensemble. All of them are wearing black. These people have style and they carry themselves with dignity. *I could fit in with them,* Zach tells himself.

The men have cases of beer and the women are clutching designer purses. They push and shove each other, laughing and play fighting. They're chatting with the valet, a chubby man from Ghana with a big smile and an even bigger laugh. Zach can hear his chuckles even though the doors are closed. He wishes he could go out there, but he has to stay at the desk. He tries not to stare, feeling it seems too desperate, yet he stares nonetheless.

When the group finally splits–one man and one woman walking away towards Michigan Avenue, the rest heading past the front desk down the hall to the elevators, and Tina still outside holding a case of beer and sucking on the tail end of her cigarette–Zach buries his head in *1984* and pretends to read.

"Mr. Winston, I presume?" She asks, trotting through the lobby with her chest puffed out and her chin held high, fiddling with an imaginary monocle; in her other hand, a case of beer. In a rather unconvincing British accent, she says, "Good day, Mr. Winston. I've brought us some ale to take the chill off this rather drafty evening. I do hope it suits you, Mr. Winston."

"Good show, old chap," Zach replies, and even he's surprised. First a smile, then a laugh, now a joke. He hasn't had this lively an evening at work in months...maybe years. "Where'd you get these?" he asks.

"I didn't even have to make a trek to the store. It turns out my mates had already purchased libations for the evening. They're fine fellows. Fine, indeed."

She opens two beers and they both froth over, but she's quick to slurp down the foam. Zach dutifully wipes off the counter. It's not long before he's drinking. He's not thinking about the cameras anymore, only the woman in front of him. He's thinking about seeing her on his day off. He's thinking about being one of the guys in her circle, and how much he'd love to go to a wedding reception and go on a beer run and play fight outside a hotel. He's thinking of seeing more of those tattoos. What's under that dress? Where does the ink trail end?

Zach hasn't met many women since he finished college. That was years ago. Women aren't interested in fine arts majors. Drawing doesn't pay for fancy dinners or a white picket fence or two and a half children. His schedule is that of a vampire's. Sleeping from 8:00am to 4:00pm isn't appealing to most human beings. The human body clock prefers moonlight and quiet for sleep.

But here's a woman in front of him. A woman who approached *him*. She's beautiful, covered in tattoos, and wants to drink with a hotel clerk at 1:30 or 2:00 or whatever ungodly hour it is. She listens to genres of metal he's never heard of. And she reads. She reads a lot. Voraciously. She prefers the Chinese food in Chinatown to the shit everywhere else. She smells like whiskey and cigarettes, and Zach is fawning over her every word.

But the best part, what sets her above any woman he's met since becoming the night auditor for the Empire Hotel, is that she's a tattoo artist.

She reaches into her bra and pulls out a wad of cash and some credit cards and a business card. She slides the business card across the front desk. *Tina Sanchez. Windy Apple Tattoos.*

"You work at this place?" Zach analyzes the card. He's checking for foul play, forgery, Photoshop. But there is none. He tucks it between the pages of his book.

"I own it." She's standing on her tiptoes with her arms crossed on the marble counter. Her chin is resting in the crook of her elbow, nonchalant, as if this is ordinary information; as if beautiful tattoo artists stumble into Zach's life every night. "I learned everything I know from my cousin," she says, but Zach has drifted off.

His mind is churning. He's coming up with schemes and scenarios, envisioning himself as a tattoo artist. What would his arms look like dressed in a sleeve? Hours of sitting around and drawing, like when he was young. Like when he was a child and he drew comic book heroes and monsters, and in high school when his friends told him he could draw tattoos. Or when he was in college and still aspired to be a comic book artist or paint portraits, whatever dream fell into his lap.

And then the visions of holding hands with Tina, closing up shop for the evening, gazing into each other's eyes. He'd leave his studio apartment to go live in her flat, where they'd read books and hold hands. They'd critique each other's drawings and review the earnings from their business venture, the Windy Apple Tattoo Parlor.

"...and if it wasn't for Benny, I'd still be sweeping floors at The Shop and Save." Her head lilts, dreamy-eyed, and she drifts off into memories. "I can't believe it's been twenty years. I was seventeen when I went off to the Bronx. Who knows what would have happened to me if

Benny hadn't offered me that apprenticeship?" Wet spots are forming around her eyes. She's smiling. Zach hands her a tissue. "I guess that's what family is for, right?"

Zach nods, but he doesn't have much of a family. His dad passed on while he was in college, and his mom lets him do his laundry at her house. That's about it.

Tina hops up onto the desk with her stomach pressed against the marble, her legs dangling in midair. She reaches across the counter, over his book, and snatches a pen off his keyboard.

"Roll up your sleeve," she says.

"What?" Zach shakes his head, returns to reality, and looks her in the face.

"Roll up your sleeve." Zach listens this time. "Now give me your arm," she says. And he does.

"What are you writing?"

"Won't take long. Give me a second."

After a minute or so, she's finished. On his arm, in thick black lettering is *Who controls the past controls the future. Who controls the present controls the past.*

"What's this?" he says.

"It's from your book. Or Rage, I suppose; whichever you prefer," she says, dropping back to the floor.

"Right. I guess I'm a little out of it. Maybe it's the beer getting to me." But he'd only taken a few sips, hardly enough to have an effect.

31

The lettering is beautiful. Thick and dark, a bit hectic, but purposefully so. Each letter comes to a sharp spike at the end. The W's look like two lightning bolts fused together. Zach is amazed that she did it so quickly, and it causes him to sink back into his imagination.

Now he's an old man, covered in ink and dotted with piercings, still as bald as he was the day he met Tina, and still wearing the glasses she fell in love with. He's in the Windy Apple Tattoo Parlor. It's small and cozy. The lights are dimmed since it's after hours, and he can almost smell the chamomile tea on the table next to his easel. He's laboring on a design, a watchful blue eye. Tina enters from the back room, carrying a cup of hot chocolate. She has a bit of a limp, and she presses her arm to her back where it aches. Her wrinkles make her face sag a bit, but her tattoos are still vibrant. She is still beautiful. "Who is that for?" she asks, and he answers, "It's for you, my dear." She grabs his hand and gives it a tight squeeze.

There's that squeeze again, firm yet gentle; so full of love. And then a jolt, a slap on the wrist. "Anybody home? Hello?"

He takes off his glasses and rubs his eyes. "Hey, can I draw something for you?" he asks.

"Sure." She hands him the pen.

"No, I mean...not right now." He takes the pen and rests it on his book. "I'm a fine arts major. Well, I *was* a fine arts major. I have a degree in illustration--"

"Toast to that!" she says. She raises her can high and waits for a response.

Zach scrambles for his drink and they clink cans together, but he doesn't take a swig. "What I'm trying to say is, since I have some experience drawing, maybe I could draw something for you."

"Maybe so," she says. She hops onto the desk again, her stomach balancing on the marble and her legs kicking in the air. She pulls her business card from his book and holds it in his face. "Stop by sometime. Bring in some work."

"Absolutely," he says.

Tina's friends, the man and woman who walked off earlier, enter through the foyer and a gust of cool air swirls around the front desk. Zach and Tina both shiver.

"What time is it?" she asks.

"Time?" He can't remember the last time he checked. Time has a way of slipping away. He checks the clock on his computer. "4:30. Holy crap. I have to get back to the audit."

"Well, I guess it's about time to hit the hay, then." She stands perfectly straight, clicks her heels, and salutes him.

He can't help but chuckle. "Good night," he says.

"Zach?"

"Yeah?"

"I had fun."

✳ ✳ ✳

A few days pass. A few cycles of 11:00 to 7:00. Complaints. Solitude. The nightly paperwork. He's only there to press buttons. He's there simply to be there, just in case. Just in case. He fixes mistakes. A bellman who forgot a piece of luggage; a maid who didn't leave enough pillows. Someone has to be there, just in case.

He has lots of free time. Time to read. He's read lots of books. Long and short. Big and small. But over the past few days since meeting Tina, he's neglected his book. It's been in his backpack the entire time, that watchful blue eye staring at him, asking why he's neglecting his most loyal companion. He's contemplated reading, he really has, but he's been busy drawing. With his eyeglasses set aside, he can only see the sketch pad in front of him. His book, the lobby, and anyone in it is a blur, a distraction.

It's been ages. At first, he had to shake off the rust. A few lines. Cross them out. A few shapes. Cross them out. Crumpled balls of paper piling up, but his sketch pad is thick, he's barely touched it in years. How many years have gone by? He can't remember. Four? Five? Six? Not seven? Has it been seven years since he graduated college? No internships to show for it. His resume only half done, still a ticking line on Word. And no pictures. No sketches. No drawings. No doodles. Nothing.

But he has free time. It's a luxury. He's good at killing time. Every once in a while, he has to stop to press a button on the computer, make sure the audit runs. Charge the guests for parking, post the nightly room charges, print reports, close out the day, let the system lie dormant for a while; all before 1:00am. Restart the system, run diagnostics, print reports, wait. These steps come after 4:00 am. There are large chunks of time in between. All he has to do is press a button. The computer knows the rest.

He draws a lot in those few days after meeting Tina. He never calls her or texts her or emails her, but he draws, preparing for a meeting. He wants to impress her. Lines become shapes, shapes become figures, and figures become many things. Lions, dragons, superheroes, flowers, skulls, faces, eyes. Big blue eyes. He draws lots of those. None of them satisfy him. None are good enough for Tina. Too many clichés. What does a unique tattoo look like? Does such a thing exist? It doesn't occur to Zach that Tina never asked him for his drawings, and she certainly didn't ask for perfection.

On the last day of this stretch of work days, he receives a text message from Tina. *Come by the shop tomorrow. 10ish, before it gets busy.* He's at the front desk. In front of him is a sketch pad, a pile of graphite pencils, charcoal pencils, and several wads of balled up paper. It's 1:00am, and he groans at the time she's chosen. 10:00. He hasn't been awake at 10:00am in months. But he has to go; he's been summoned. He has no offering. He has no drawing to present to her;

nothing he hasn't thrown away; nothing to prove his worth, but he's been summoned. He has to go.

✳ ✳ ✳

His alarm sounds like an air raid siren. EENK EENK EENK EENK EENK. He slaps at it, but it's still screeching. EENK EENK EENK EENK EENK. 9:45am. He's hit the snooze three times already. He sacrificed a shower, breakfast, and a cup of coffee. He hits it one more time; now he's sacrificing punctuality.

He wakes up at 10:30, bleary eyed; his head tingling. It's a side effect of sleep deprivation. He feels this way almost daily, but he's still not used to it. He never will be. It's hard to sleep during the day; hard to adjust. Too much sound. There's construction and neighbors and babies and dogs. Too much light. No matter how thick his curtains are, his bedroom still faces east. He's still not used to it, even after years of working overnight.

Fortunately, the morning is gray and overcast, rainy, so at least his eyes are at ease.

A bell above the front door rings as he enters the Windy Apple Tattoo Parlor. It smells like a hospital. Rubbing alcohol, disinfectant. It's too clean. The floors reflect the florescent lights on the ceiling. They're buffed to a sheen. Everything is so clean. So bright.

There's music coming from somewhere. He can't see the speakers, but he knows the song. It's Rage Against the Machine. *Who controls the past now controls the future. Who controls the present now controls the past.* But the smell doesn't match. The song is too powerful. God, that smell. So sterile. So empty. *Now, testify! It's right outside your door, now testify!*

The receptionist is busy with a magazine. She's leaning against the counter, bobbing her head to the song. She looks fragile, tiny wrists and a collarbone that juts out. She has short blonde hair, a thick, bull's horn of a nose ring, and a few scattered tattoos on her forearms. If Zach saw her on the street, he might think she was cute, but combined with that hospital smell, she looks like an oncology patient, fragile and dormant. Barely human at all.

He heads to the counter and stands there until the receptionist speaks to him. "Can I help you?" she says.

"I'm here to see Tina," he says. The receptionist is staring at him. It's jarring. Is it the bags under his eyes? Or maybe that he's wearing sweat pants?

He can't look her in the eye, so he stares at her magazine, *Apartment Finder.* "Are you the bride?" he asks. It's an attempt to lighten the mood. "I work at the Empire Hotel."

"My suite was terrible," the receptionist says. Her lip curls up on one side and she looks Zach up and down before she lets out a "hmph." She points at Tina. "She's back there." And she's back to searching for apartments.

"So, do I just...do I just go back there?"

37

"Duh," she says.

He's too tired to be disgusted by this woman, so he says nothing.

That first step from the waiting area, past the counter, into the inner sanctum is the hardest. It's like opening an "employees only" door. He feels like he's breaking the rules. He hasn't earned the right to enter this area.

Tina finally notices him. "Zach! How's it going?" She reclines in her chair and waves him towards her. "Don't be shy. Nothing to be afraid of."

She's sitting in the last chair all the way in the back, and she's eating a hot dog. It's so nice to see her eating a hot dog. It looks human. It's down to earth, blue collar. She's not so sterile, after all.

Without leaving her big leather chair–the kind a dentist might use–she swivels towards the wall and turns a knob to kill the music. The discordant mismatch of rubbing alcohol and Rage Against the Machine is gone, but now it's just silent, and he's surprised that he wants the music back.

"Nice place."

She pops out of her chair and punches him in the arm. "Thanks, buddy."

She looks older. She's not wearing makeup, and she has crow's feet. She wears a black bowler hat and her hair is tucked underneath instead of flowing to her shoulders. She's wearing a blue denim jacket, so he can't even see her tattoos. And her eyes...they're not blue, but brown; dull and ordinary. He hardly recognizes her, but at least he knows she's human, because her hands are shimmering with grease and mustard stains and her breath smells like meat.

"Hold on a second," she says. She disappears into a door near her chair. There's water running, and then she steps out with a toothbrush in her mouth. There's foam around her lips. She heads over to her chair and bends down to dig through her purse. She pops back up with hand sanitizer, and heads back to the washroom to spit and rinse. When she returns, she's rubbing the alcohol into her palms.

"Sorry about that. This place has to be spotless." She pulls a bottle of disinfectant and sprays down her chair, buffing the leather until it shines.

Zach nods, but his hand is clenched tight. This isn't the woman he remembers from a few nights earlier.

"Did that *bitch*," she screams the word, "give you any trouble?"

The receptionist flips Tina the bird without looking up from her magazine.

"She's not very friendly," Zach says.

"She's a teddy bear. She's just salty because she snoozed on a bargain. Studio in Bucktown, only $1,300 a month, right near the train, too."

$1,300 a month sounds like a lot to Zach. He pays $800 a month for a studio, and he still struggles. But his place isn't near the train, and it isn't in Bucktown. There are no boutiques or organic food restaurants in his neighborhood, and even if there were, he couldn't afford them. His place is a small single-unit on the seventh floor of a crumbling redbrick complex with a bed, a bathroom, and a kitchenette. He has a poster of Zack de la Rocha, a few graphite sketches from college, and books strewn about the floor. Hardly enough to even tell someone lives there. Not much of a bargain in Zach's mind.

"There's a position opening up," Tina says. She punches him in the arm again, in the same spot, except this time it hurts. "Ms. Friendly is moving on up, and I'm looking to replace her."

There's a feeling of elation somewhere inside Zach. He's barely able to recognize it, but it's there. He's sleepy and his head is tingling and his vision is blurry despite his glasses, but a smile inches across his face, and somewhere inside–maybe in his gut, he can't tell–there's something like happiness.

Tina disappears again, this time through a door next to the washroom marked, "Employees Only." There are a few crashes, curses, the sound of water filling something metal, and then she's back, this time with a bucket. It has casters on the bottom, and inside is a bowl of water and bubbly soap with a broom sticking out the end.

"What's this?" Zach asks, half hoping this is for the receptionist and not him.

"A job interview," she says.

He puts little effort into his work, making broad swoops with the mop. He's not sure why he didn't object. He just couldn't say no to her, at least not to her face; he certainly doesn't want to mop the floor. There's a scrub brush in the bucket as well, but he doesn't touch it. He shoves the broom back and forth. It's already too clean, but he keeps going in no particular pattern. He moves from one chair to the next, eight chairs total. Tina doesn't have any appointments this early, so she watches him. "You missed a spot," she says. The floor is so shiny and the lights are so bright that it's easy to see where he's half-assing the job, which is most everywhere.

When he finishes mopping around the last chair up front by the receptionist, he leaves the bucket and heads back to Tina sitting in her chair by the back. "Is that good?"

"You're not interested?" she says.

"What do you mean?"

"Come on, Zach." Her arms are crossed and there's a bemused grin on her face. "That was pathetic."

For a moment, Zach wants nothing more than to tip over her chair and watch her spill onto the floor. He didn't ask to mop the floor. Is it because he didn't bring a sketch? There must be a reason she's treating him like a pawn. He came to see her because she asked, because she owns her own business, because she has beautiful black hair with blonde tips and a tight black dress and two full sleeves of ink and defiant blue eyes. He didn't come for a mop and a fucking bucket.

She leans forward and snaps her fingers in his face. "Hello? Fine arts degree, are you there? Tina Sanchez here. Earth to Zach?"

"I'm really tired. I didn't get much sleep."

Tina nods. "I can respect that. I worked overnight for a while. Helped pay the rent when I was apprenticing with my cousin Benny. He only paid minimum wage, fucking prick, but I wouldn't be here without him."

Minimum wage. Is that what she'd pay him? He heard her say it, but it sounded so far away, like a television turned down just a hair above mute. Minimum wage. She called it an apprenticeship, but it sounds like indentured servitude. He'd still have to work overnight at the hotel. How else would he pay the rent? How else would he pay for groceries? Gas? Electricity? Seven years since he'd finished college, and he still hadn't made a dent in his student loans. Minimum wage wouldn't work.

It couldn't possibly work. He'd have to work overnight, but he'd get even less sleep. She'd want him to come in at 10:00am, maybe earlier. When would he sleep? Not at work. The beers he drank at work the other night hadn't washed away his fear of the cameras, and he'd never get any reading done, not to mention the tingling sensation behind his eyes. That comes from lack of sleep, and the last thing he needed to do is exacerbate it. He already lives in a fog; two jobs won't clear that away.

"Zach, are you interested?" She stands up, holds both of his hands, and looks into his eyes. "If you don't want the job, that's fine. I'm perfectly fine being your friend instead of your boss." She squeezes his hands, but they're limp. "I'm here all the time, always working. I don't get out much, so I...I don't meet many guys I like."

But Zach's oblivious. "I just...I..." He rubs his eyes, shakes his head, and tries to give her his full attention, but he's not all there. "I need to sleep on it. I need some time."

He looks at his wrist, as if there's a watch there. He doesn't know what time it is or how much of it he needs to make a decision. He heads back towards the entrance and notices a clock above the door. 12:30pm. He doesn't know how long he can keep her waiting. She'll need an answer. He's not even sure what the question was. All he knows is that his eyes hurt and it's his day off and there's a bed waiting for him at home. He knows that despite the hour, he'll wake up at 4:00pm like he always does, tired and groggy. He knows that Tina won't wait forever; that sooner or later, she'll need a decision.

But once he gets home and his head hits the pillow, he's made his decision–even if he doesn't know it. He wakes at 4:00pm on a Monday–he knows it's Monday because it's his day off–and pours himself into his drawings, trying his best to ignore the incessant tingling behind his eyes. Tuesday, Wednesday, Thursday. A few drawings get done, but most wind up in the trash. Weeks go by. The drawings grow fewer and fewer, and he finds himself spending more and more time in his book. *Why aren't you reading?* the watchful blue eye asks him, but he doesn't have an answer.

When Winston Smith met a girl, things went terribly wrong for him, so maybe it's for the best that he hasn't sent Tina even a single text. Eventually, he realizes it's been more than a month–it's May or June–

and he still hasn't given her an answer. It's probably too late, and *1984* is a good book, and there's rent to pay. *It's definitely too late,* he thinks.

He's wasted too much time.

Take My Breath Away

Don't waste oxygen, not a single breath. Nothing is more precious. Nothing is more expensive. Treasure it. Conserve it. Breathe in through the nose. Take it slow. Hold it in your lungs. Savor it. Remove the mask ever so slightly and close the valve. Waste nothing. Breathe out.

It was routine to Juniper, just the way she'd learned from her mother. An old mantra she'd held onto since her youth. It had gotten them through the worst of the Dust Lung, back when a man would kill his brother for a tank of oxygen. You had to hold onto what you had, or you wouldn't have it for long. Some things never changed. Lessons she'd learned ages ago still served her well.

Now she had a career, a home, and a husband. They were all modest, but to her younger self it was extravagant to even dream of them. She clutched the faded upholstery of her Barcalounger, taking in a bit of the good canned air she needed to make it through her day. A long hit of pure oxygen eased her nerves. It was more for her soul than her body. It was the one luxury she allowed herself, for there were so few in her life.

The lights of the city skyline filtered in through her blinds, casting a golden glow over the apartment. The gaudiness of Futurus galled her, but it helped to hide the cracks and chipped paint of her tired apartment. She tried to cover the wear and tear with carefully placed curtains and Ricky's charcoal sketches, but on one income, it was all they could afford.

She took one more pull form the tank. "Don't talk to me before I've had my oxygen," Ricky would always say. She'd laugh no matter how times he said it, but it always rang so true. She just couldn't start her day without it.

Once her lungs had their fill, she checked the tarp over the windows to make sure there were no new tears. They'd need a new tarp soon, but it wasn't something she had the energy to think about so early. She pulled the blinds shut and headed off to the restroom to get ready for the day.

She balanced her professionalism with a hint of her personality. Her job paid the bills, but she was still **Ms. Juniper**. The bohemians of the Vesper district's lounge scene still remembered her, and she felt a need to live up to that ideal of herself, even if it was no longer a part of her life. She slipped into a black dress with ruffled trim; even on a budget, she still wanted to keep up with the fashion. She wore bright red lipstick because the Inspector General of Air Purity was a flirt and she could wiggle a few extra filters out of him. She pinned her hair up with a black ribbon as an homage to her favorite contralto, Ambrosia Red.

The white-haired woman in the mirror never ceased to amaze her. She remembered when her hair had been red, before the days of the dust. She was just a girl then. There were so many vibrant colors in those days. Reds, blondes, brunettes, and blacks; so many shades in

46

between. Now, only the city's richest could afford dyes or vintage wigs to escape the stark white. Futurus took everything, even the color of her hair.

She sighed and finished her morning routine, then moved to the wall terminal to call a cab. She had to bash the old clunker with her purse to stop its flickering, and even then, it hummed a staticky green. If she could afford to replace it she would, but it was either that or Ricky's oxygen tanks.

"Hey Jun, you're not thinking of leaving without saying goodbye to your number one fella?"

"Of course not, dear. I'll be right there." Ricky was looking a bit paler than she liked. She spent everything she had to get him the best oxygen available. She had a ventilator and fresh masks at the ready whenever he needed. She even got him one of the fancy televisions that connected to the city's data networks. He spent most of his day cooped up in bed, so the least she could do was make sure he had a bit of entertainment.

"Give your little Lime Ricky a kiss." He pulled back his mask and she gave him a light peck on the lips. She wanted to hold the kiss a bit longer like they used to, but he didn't have the lungs for it anymore.

"I have a short shift today, so I'll be back in no time."

"Don't mind me. The Schooners are playing today. Old man Roth's pitching."

"All right, then. I'm off to ventilate the masses."

Ricky smiled, but she could see the sadness behind it. "Don't you ever think about going back to the Vesper, picking up the microphone again? It's so rare to find a set of pipes like yours, Jun."

"You know we can't afford that."

"I can go back to the factory. I'll get a portable tank. I still got it, babe."

She hugged him so tight. Her beautiful Ricky. Of course, he would go back to work for her. All she had to do was ask. It would kill him, but he'd do it in a heartbeat.

"Let me carry the load for a while," she said, kissing him on the cheek. With that, she was off before he could muster an argument.

❋ ❋ ❋

The sky was dark, as usual. It was so rare that the sun pierced the dust. Black swirls rose up and down the streets, leaving trails of soot. But even without the sun, the city glowed a lavish gold. The skyscrapers that dominated the skyline were dotted with lights that ran in intricate swirls, chevrons, and the ever-popular sunburst motif. The rich golden hues coursed through the city like veins of molten ore.

You could tell how much oxygen a building was getting by how brightly it glowed. Hers was a dim bit of brick and crumbling mortar, but the horizon was full of shimmering goliaths.

The cab passed by the great corporate towers, Magnacore, Kepler and Kepler, Vergamax, and Dovian. Their sharp edges and decorative spires pierced the sky like knives. Their ornate trim and latticework was a reminder of where the wealth was concentrated. Juniper hated it; so garish and ostentatious. It was beautiful on the outside, but empty within. Their lights shimmered against the swirls of black dust while the city below suffocated. Her Ricky suffocated.

The cab pulled up to the Futurus Memorial Conservatory. She slipped on her gas mask before tapping her credit chit to the cabbie's console. A gust of the dust pushed against her as she stepped out of the cab. She shook it from her hair, but even trace amounts kept each strand Futurus White.

She crossed over Memorial Bridge, which spanned what used to be the Futurus Canal. The water had been drained ages ago, and now it was just a shantytown for the sick and homeless. She tried not to stare, but she wondered how any of them survived walking the streets without masks. They had shirts and towels wrapped around their face, but nothing that could really keep it out. The tragedy of those walking corpses wore on her, and she hurried across the bridge, keeping her eyes on her feet. Men, women, and children in tattered rags shuffled by beneath them, roasting meats of presumably questionable origins. The sounds of their hacking and wheezing was too much to bear, so she hummed one of Ambrosia's hits.

"It's the little things that get you through it." The sounds were muffled and tinny through the rebreather of her mask, but, as the song said, the little things.

On the other side of the bridge was the Conservatory, the home to the Futurus oxygen supply. The Lungs of Futurus, people called it. It was the only thing she found beautiful in the whole city, aside from her Ricky. The massive domed structure was made of reinforced fiberglass, shimmering bright white against the gold ingots that Futurus called buildings. Its smooth lines and curves stood out in stark contrast to the harsh spiked edges of the skyscrapers. Ricky always called it a breath of fresh air. She smiled at the thought.

The main gate was heavily guarded. Armed soldiers stood watch and snipers perched along the perimeter of the dome. Citizens from all districts of Futurus flocked to the Conservatory's great gardens. Even the hard laborers of the Barley District saved up for the occasional trip. All of them were patted down at the main gate. Even as an employee she couldn't escape the humiliation. They scanned her badge and waved her through.

Once inside, she slipped off her mask and breathed in fresh air the way it was meant to be enjoyed. The Conservatory was rich with plant life. There really was no air like it anywhere in the city. It smelled of soil and greenery, and she started each shift by soaking it in. It wasn't the life she wanted, but it paid well enough to care for Ricky and gave her the opportunity to soak in the best air in the world on a daily basis, so it wasn't all bad.

She punched the clock and made her way past the reception bot. "Good day, Inspector Juniper." She nodded and made her way to the deciduous temperate wing. She pulled her air purity reader from her purse and began her scans. The machine's gears and motors spun into action, sending lines of code and data spilling out onto the screen. It whirred in her hand, sending a slight vibration up her arm.

"101.325 kPa. 21% oxygen," she mumbled to herself.

"Hey there, toots."

She looked up and saw the conservatory's chief of maintenance, a greasy little man with a limp that she assumed was classic Barley district affectation at its worst. He ogled her breasts as he sidled up to her, and she was immediately reminded why she hated him so dearly.

"Mr. Groslch." Juniper walked straight past, not bothering to look him in the eye, but of course, he followed.

"You're with me tonight, little lady."

"I was told Mr. Collins would be accompanying me."

"Tom's busy putting together the Garden Gala. We're stuck with each other." He gave her a playful jab with his elbow that left her feeling the need to bathe.

They made their rounds through the Conservatory. The readings were on target. The temperate deciduous and coniferous zones were spot on, as was the boreal zone. Air production was at peak performance, and the processing and distribution plants were operating at optimal standards. It would have been a fine shift if not for Grolsch leering at her behind the entire time.

When they came to the tropical zone, the last stop on her rounds, she found something amiss. The air felt perfectly fine, but without her equipment, she never would have noticed the slight dip in quality and flow.

"Tropical zone readings are inadequate. Barometric pressure is below normal standards." She pulled a pen and a notepad and began taking notes. "This is a breach of protocol. I'll have to file a report."

"Yeah, we're having a bit of trouble with the regulators. Should be fixed by the end of the month." Grolsch took a step far too close for Juniper's liking.

"That's unacceptable. They need to be in order by the end of the day. Do I have to report you to Curator Collins?" He was in her personal space, but she wouldn't be intimidated. She stood tall and looked him straight in the eye.

"They're his orders," Grolsch said as he pushed his finger into her shoulder. "Madame Inspector."

She wanted to slap him. Her mother would have told her to put him on his ass, but instead she said, "Then maybe I'll report Curator Collins to the Bureau of Air Purity. I wonder how they'll respond to substandard air flow in the Vesper District."

"Listen, toots. Truth is, Tom had me route the airflow into the grand ballroom. They're making a big push with the donors this month so those freeloaders in the Vesper can go fuck themselves." He slipped a big wad of cash from his pocket and shoved it into the strap of her bra.

"That's a gift from the Curator. You keep your mouth shut and this'll be a good month for you."

He walked away before she could respond. A scream bubbled up in the back of her throat that she only narrowly stifled. Slimy men like Grolsch were the grease that kept Futurus running. She hated playing their game, but she couldn't lose her job. She couldn't force Ricky back to the steel mill. Some people made it through the Dust Lung; it was possible, and Ricky was a fighter. Ambrosia Red did it; so could he. He wouldn't work a day until the doctor's said his lungs were clear.

She bit her tongue and didn't give Grolsch the satisfaction.

Her shift was over, and she couldn't have been more grateful for anything in the world. She slid her ticket into the time clock and it pinged with its familiar message, "A hard day's labor!" The screen lit up with a little green lightshow meant to resemble fireworks as her credit balance rose. It was always a treat to watch the display. Not only did it mean she was getting paid, but it meant she could finally go home for the day.

Just as she was about to slip on her mask and coat, someone called her name. "Ms. Juniper, excuse me. Might I have a word?"

She turned to find the Conservatory's curator trotting up to her. Thomas Collins. She'd thought well of him when they first met. He was polite and cordial enough, but the incident with Grolsch wasn't the first;

she'd grown to see Collins as being just as ugly. The difference was that Collins knew how to hide it.

"Mr. Collins."

"Please, you know I prefer Tom."

"How can I help you, Tom?"

Collins urged Juniper to follow him, gesturing back towards the Conservatory proper like an usher at the Grand Futurus Opera House.

She stood perfectly still. "My shift is over. I was just about to leave."

"Mr. Grolsch told me about your discussion. I'm wondering..."

"Yes," she interrupted. "I'll keep quiet. I can alter the readings, but it will cost you more."

"Of course. You'll find I'm a charitable man." He started off back into the Conservatory. "If you'll follow me Inspector, I assure you it will be worth your while."

He led her to the Conservatory's private celebration area, the Chambord Memorial Gardens. They stood outside the wrought iron gates that led into the main garden. Grolsch had mentioned a gala, but Juniper hadn't pictured anything so extravagant. Golden bulbs lit the garden's pathways and mirrored the skyscraper's veins. Above them hung gold streamers that paralleled the walkways. The tables, the chairs, and the bar were also gold. Even the servers wore gold bow ties and vests in contrast to the black trim of their jackets. It was like the whole event had been touched by King Midas himself.

At the center of the garden was a stage that like everything else, was dripping in gold. The stage was set with two guitars, a piano, and a microphone so big and garish it couldn't help but be noticed, even amongst the sea of golden trinkets.

"Our guests will be arriving soon," Collins said, "and we have a bit of a problem. You see, our main vocalist has come down with the Dust Lung, and well, you know how that wreaks havoc on one's voice."

"I should be getting home, my husband--" She turned to walk away, but he grabbed her by the shoulder.

"I've heard you're a four-octave singer."

"I really..."

"You had a bit of a following not so long ago, didn't you? Mr. Grolsch says he saw you perform at Campari Alley. He described your voice as husky..."

"It's not--"

"...but with a wide range. I don't mean to pigeonhole you, my dear."

"I don't do that anymore."

"You will be *very* well compensated for the evening."

She sighed and took in a deep breath.

"It's just one night," he said.

"I'll need to see the figures in writing."

"Of course, Madame Inspector. Of course." He ushered her off again, and this time she followed without delay. "Now if you'll follow me to the dressing room, we'll need to get you into something a bit more...elegant."

✳ ✳ ✳

The dressing room was decorated far less grand than the gala. Collins practically shoved her into the little stone walled room. There was a table, a mirror rimmed with lights, a chair, and little else.

Collins stood outside, yelling through the room's thick door. "Your predecessor's dress is waiting for you. I do hope it fits."

A gold sequined dress hung from the mirror and a pair of matching gold heels rested on the table. It was beautiful, she had to admit. She held it against her body, taking a mental picture before trying it on. She hadn't worn anything like it in years.

And there she was, five years earlier, in a dress just like this one, up on stage with Monsieur Burgundy on the keys at the Hurricane Club. The crowd was running hot, all the fellas slipping off their jackets and loosening their ties. They had that good old-time oxygen back then, so she could hit the real big notes. They ate up every bar, every measure. Ambrosia Red was in the audience that night, and even she was impressed, but...

"Has it really been that long?" she said to herself.

"You're free to sing whatever you'd like. Our band is extraordinarily well-versed, so you needn't worry about obscurity."

"Maybe this won't be so bad." She was careful not to let Collins hear her, didn't want to give him the satisfaction.

She slipped off her clothes and slid into the dress. It was a bit too tight, but nothing she couldn't handle. She hopped and wiggled, inching the dress up over her curves.

"You know, if all goes well tonight," he said through the door, "we may be able to make this a recurring arrangement."

The dress was more revealing than she would have liked. It showed off too much cleavage and it hugged her behind like plastic wrap. She tugged and prodded, trying to make it decent, but it was meant to show off. She felt like a glass of champagne, something to be paraded about for a special occasion and then forgotten.

"How does that sound?"

There was no way out at that point. "Just enjoy the music," she whispered to herself. "You get to sing tonight. You're getting paid to sing. Try to enjoy it."

"Are you almost ready?" He knocked a few times. "Ms. Juniper? It's almost time."

She opened the door and turned her back to him. "Zip me up."

Collins obliged, trying his best not to blush. "I do hope you'll consider my offer."

"We'll see."

The crowd turned to get a look at her the moment she stepped through the gate. The spotlight had yet to find her, but they gawked nonetheless. She kept her eyes on her feet. It had been so long since she'd been on stage, and this didn't feel the same. When she sang at The Coupe, it was old friends from college; at The Tumbler, it was fellow singers and performers; at The Rocks, it was the real music lovers. But these people. She had no idea who they were. "Bunch of rich leaches," she said to her golden shoes.

"And now, ladies and gentlemen, please welcome to the stage the ravishing Ms. Juniper." The spotlight came up and her sequins twinkled like diamonds.

They were already staring, so she decided to forego any gestures to acknowledge their gawking. She made her way to stage, taking in the band's setup. There were three men in tuxedos waiting to greet her. The two guitarists were both tall and skinny. One had short hair dyed black and a thick but neatly trimmed mustache. The other had long spiked hair dyed gold. The man at the piano wore thick-framed sunglasses, and despite his thinning hair that was dyed a simple light brown, he was quite handsome.

When she reached the stage, the mustachioed man held out his hand and helped her up. "I'm Freddie, this is David, and that's Elton. Anything you need, dear, do let us know. The Curator informed us of your song choice. We're ready when you are."

"Thank you."

Freddie's genuine kindness was the boost she needed; she could do this. She spotted an oxygen tank under the piano and decided to take a pull before singing. The oxygen rushed into her lungs and the strength of it buoyed her.

"It's just one night," she said to herself.

She stepped to the mic and looked out over the crowd. They were as lush and garish as the décor in their tailored suits and mink coats. They had hair dyed shades of blue and purple, red and orange, green and gold. She loathed them at first sight, but they were her crowd and she would give them a good show.

"This song is called *Take My Breath Away*." Juniper took up the song. "Oooooooooh Ooooooooh."

Her vocalists followed suit. "Ooooooooh Oooooh. Take it, take it all away."

"Ooooooooooooooooooooooh Ooooooooooooh."

"Ooooh Ooooh, Take my breath awaaaaaaaay."

She sat atop the piano and let the song take over. "Look into my eyes and you'll see...I'm the only one." It had been years, but the old muscles showed no rust. "You've captured my love...stolen my heart...changed my life." It was as though she'd never stopped. "Every time you make a move...you destroy my mind...and the way you touch...I lose control and shiver...deep inside." For a moment, she couldn't remember why she'd ever quit. There was nothing in the world but the song. "You take my breath away."

The audience felt the passion of it as much as Juniper. "You can reduce me to tears with a single sigh." She felt the connection that only music created. "Every breath that you take...any sound that you make...is a whisper in my ear." She locked eyes with a couple in the front row. They were a handsome pair. The man was tall with a neat black goatee and the woman's dark inky hair fell past the small of her back.

"I could give up all my life for just one kiss...I would surely die...if you dismiss me from your love." They held hands and she could see they were enamored. They looked into each other's eyes and smiled. The sight of them unnerved her and she looked away.

"You take my breath away." The couple never took their eyes off her. She could feel their gaze like a palpable presence. "So please don't go...don't leave me here all by myself...I get ever so lonely from time to time." The man called Curator Collins to his table and whispered something in his ear.

"I will find you...anywhere you go...I'll be right behind you...right until the ends of the earth." She couldn't look at them any longer. She closed her eyes and escaped into the song. "I will find you...anywhere you go...I'll be right behind you...right until the ends of the earth." "To tell you that you juuuuuuuuust...You take my breath away."

When she opened her eyes, they were still staring. "I will find you...anywhere you go...right until the ends of the earth." They frightened her. She wanted to run screaming back to Ricky. "I'll get no sleep 'til I find you to tell you when I've found you."

60

She closed her eyes again and this time, she pictured her husband. She pictured Ricky sitting alone in the audience, dancing and tapping the table to the beat like he always did when she performed. She saw that look of pride and adoration; joy and love; and just a hint of lust. She missed her husband so deeply she feared she'd never see him again, and tears rolled down her cheeks.

"I love yoooooooooooooou." She carried the last note longer than normal. She couldn't help it. It was the only thing that made sense at the moment.

The crowd stood up and burst into uproarious applause. They whistled and cheered, and the clapping seemed to go on forever.

"Thank you," she said, wiping tears from her eyes. She sang a few more songs, but none of them carried her the way the first had. The crowd loved them, but she felt as though she were someone else masquerading as Juniper. For the life of her she just couldn't find joy in any of it.

And that couple. They leered at her. It was worse than Grolsch. Their stares made her skin crawl. They rubbed each other's hands, never taking their eyes off Juniper. The second she finished her last song, she thanked the crowd and practically ran back to the dressing room.

She slammed the door shut and breathed harsh, ragged breaths, trying to stave off a fit of hyperventilation. Her hands were shaking, and she pounded her fist on the door rather than feel so weak.

People stared and ogled; it was nothing new. She'd been on stage before, but there was something different about these two. They looked at her like she was a trophy to mount on the wall; a little golden woman to add to their collection.

She let out a scream. It was enough. "Deep breath in. Deep breath out. Let the air steady you." More tricks from her mother. *If you can control the air you breathe, then you're in control,* she used to say. Her breathing steadied and the trembling in her hands subsided.

"It was just one night. That was it. It's over." She was in control again. "Ricky's at home. Ricky's waiting."

She peeled off the golden dress and slipped back into her clothes. As she was about to put on her top, a knock came on the door.

"Ms. Juniper," Collins said, opening the door before she could answer.

"Jesus Christ, Collins!" She wasn't fully dressed. She covered herself and turned her back to him, pulling her top over her head.

"I'm sorry. I'm so sorry, my dear, but this simply cannot wait."

Once her shirt was on, she turned and waited for whatever bullshit Collins had for her. "What do you want, Tom?"

"You were marvelous. Stupendous. This night was serendipitous."

"Glad you liked it."

"Liked it? Dear, I loved it. I can't imagine why you haven't pursued a career as a songstress."

"I have obligations."

Collins laughed, waving off her obligations like a pesky fly. "Obligations, nonsense. I won't hear of it. Whatever the inspection board pays you, I'll double it. This is your calling, my dear."

"I'll consider it. Now, please leave. I'm done for the night."

"There is...one other matter." He smiled sheepishly and rubbed his chin. "You made quite the impression tonight. You're familiar with the Peychaud twins?"

"That's who they are!" The name hit her like a punch in the gut. She knew that lecherous pair was familiar. Of course, they would be from a lineage so corrupt and disgusting. "The mayor's brats."

"One and the same. Sazerac and Chartreuse." Juniper watched him rub the back of his neck and she knew he was going to say something sure to piss her off. "It seems they've taken a fancy to you."

She pounded her fist on the wall and the trembling returned.

"They'd like your...company...just for the evening."

"Leave. Now." Her breathing grew heavy and raspy and she wished she had an oxygen tank. One good hit would steady her. "Get out!"

"I realize it's a lot to ask."

"A lot to ask!" She shoved him, pushing him towards the door. He put up a meager resistance, but her rage fueled her and gave her more strength than she knew she was capable of. "It's a whole hell of lot more than a lot to ask!"

"Please hear me out." She tried to slam the door in his face, but he pushed against her.

"Get. Out!"

"You'll be well compensated. Better than your day job. Better than the performance."

"I don't want their fucking money!"

They both leaned their shoulders into the door, trying to push the other back. Juniper was winning. She nearly had the door shut, but Collins managed to sneak in his foot just at the last minute. She slammed the door on it, but he only winced. He did not scream.

"Not money, dear. Oxygen. Double your current intake. Routine filter maintenance. The finest canned air. Even a selection of fauna from the conservatory."

Juniper couldn't control her breathing. The hyperventilation hit her so hard that it brought her to her knees.

"Oxygen," she squeaked through clipped breaths.

Collins ran off and came back a moment later with a fresh tank. He held the mask to her face and she breathed in, hard and fast at first, then slower. She was wasting the air. Even though it wasn't hers, she couldn't bear the thought of it. She had to remind herself of her mantra. *Don't waste oxygen, not a single breath. Nothing is more precise. Nothing is more expensive. Treasure it. Conserve it. Breathe in through the nose. Take it slow. Hold it in your lungs. Savor it. Remove the mask ever so slightly and close the valve. Waste nothing. Breathe out.*

Her breathing returned to normal. "Good. Good," Collins said. He helped her to her feet, keeping the mask pressed over her mouth and nose. He held her hands in his and for a moment she almost forgot what a duplicitous man he was. It was as though he actually cared. "It's more than anyone has the right to ask, but they're offering a lifetime's supply of the richest oxygen."

The richest oxygen money could buy. Filter maintenance. Her own plants, in her home! It was far too lavish to dream. The thought of it was beyond her. She'd never had such luxury in all her life. She'd never even wanted it. She was content with her hovel, so long as she had Ricky.

She could, however, imagine what a doubled intake of the city's finest oxygen would do for her husband. People did survive the Dust Lung. Ricky had lived five years with the disease. He could be saved. It was rare, but it happened. Her mother had lived six years before it took her. And Ambrosia Red. Not only did she survive, but she came back with a voice stronger than when she'd left. It changed her from a soprano to a contralto, but she fought through and remade herself through sheer force of will.

Her Ricky might survive.

"It's only one night," Collins said.

"It's only one night," she repeated.

It was well past midnight. Juniper stood outside the Templeton Tower, the largest scraper in the city and home to the city's wealthiest power elites. There were air jets over the foyer's awning that blew the dust away with gale force winds so the rich and powerful could step into their limos without the nuisance of putting on a mask.

In the elevator, she practiced her breathing, keeping a calm, steady rhythm so she wouldn't slip into another fit of hyperventilation. The glass wall of the elevator looked out on the city. The dust was thick, and she could barely see the skyline aside from a bright golden outline. The floors ticked by. 20, 30, 40. She'd never been so high in her life. 50, 60, 70. It passed above the dust and she looked out on a clear night sky for the first time in her life. She'd never seen the city's golden glow except through the fog of the dust. It was so beautiful. It was so ugly.

80, 90, 100. The elevator dinged at the top floor and opened to a marble hallway leading straight ahead. Floor to ceiling windows lined the hallway. She could see the entire city. It had never seemed so small before. Along the windows were pedestals that held small bonsai trees, neatly groomed and gorgeous. Each of them surely cost more than she'd made in her entire life.

She made her way down the hall towards a set of black double doors with golden griffins etched into the wood. The griffins' talons held the knockers. She chose to rap her knuckles on the wood rather than touch the gaudy things.

Chartreuse and Sazerac each opened one of the double doors. They stood in the doorway wearing matching robes of jet black silk.

"We knew we had to have you..."

"...from the moment we saw you."

They shared a glance, transfixed on each other for a moment.

"Your voice is a triumph."

"Your song is exquisite."

"Your every breath is a gift."

"You deserve all the oxygen in the world."

"We would rip it from the lungs of the undeserving for you."

"After tonight, you breathe easy."

"You breathe easy."

Juniper's breathes grew ragged for a moment. Sazerac reached behind the door and handed her a golden tank of oxygen.

Don't waste oxygen, not a single breath. Nothing is more precise. Nothing is more expensive. Treasure it. Conserve it. Breathe in through the nose. Take it slow. Hold it in your lungs. Savor it. Remove the mask ever so slightly and close the valve. Waste nothing. Breathe out.

She turned down their oxygen tank in favor of a different lesson from her mother. *If you can control the air you breathe, then you're in control.*

They held the doors open for her and bowed to her like she was royalty.

She took in one last deep breath. "It's only one night."   She stepped inside, and the doors slammed shut behind her.

The Shadow Merchants

Luciano always died. No matter what variables we factored in. Whether we were there or not. He died in a thousand miserable ways in every multiverse. I'd seen the projections play out, and in them, I'd watched him die at the hands of bandits, tigers, starvation, exhaustion, mutiny, and sickness. I'd seen him die at sea and on land. He'd died violently, painlessly, alone, and courageously. In most cases, he died fighting, but in few desperate situations, he'd even chosen suicide.

I begged the captain to find a multiverse that left him alive, but none such existed. He scanned and scanned and scanned and found nothing. And even if he had, we could never justify such a significant change to the timeline. We'd risk being hunted down by the Time Minders. There was no way around it. Luciano always died; he had to die. He always had, and no matter what we did, he always would.

So why did I feel so guilty?

"My prince, preparations for today's journey are nearly complete."

We were so close to the rendezvous and the shame was building. We hadn't even committed the crime--if you can even call it that--but it was already eating at me.

With the rise of the sun, I flipped on the transceiver in my pendant to signal the crew that we'd be on our way soon. There was just the matter of the prince's morning routine, and then we'd be off.

The sun would crest over the dunes and he'd saunter out of the royal tent with a yawn, a stretch, and a smile. He scoffed at the idea of wearing regal attire in the desert. Instead, he chose the loose robes of the locals. His advisors insisted he at least wear the royal gold, but other than that concession, he dressed much like the guides and camp followers. The sun had tanned him so thoroughly that you might have mistaken him for a particularly wealthy local, at least if not for that bushy blonde mop atop his head.

Each day began with an inspection of his collection. "How fares my newest pet?" he said to his Master of Beasts.

He'd set out on this ill-fated journey to scour the world for riches. As the youngest son of a royal family, he was destined for the priesthood, but Luciano shirked tradition and set out on a grand treasure hunt that spanned three continents. He had a caravan full of gold and diamonds, rare weapons, exotic spices and herbs, and textiles from a dozen lands. He took great pride in the bounty he'd collected, but above all, he loved his beasts.

"She suffers in the desert heat." The Master of Beasts bowed to Luciano, but the prince stepped right past him towards the cage of a panting Bengal tiger.

The prince's personal guard, Laurel, came to his side and stood at attention. "Your highness, the caravan is ready to depart."

"But our newest member is not." The prince leaned in and addressed the tiger directly. "I know this journey is a cruel test for you, but I promise you will find my zoo much more agreeable than those wretched mummers. There are no whips under my patronage."

The tiger licked its lips and let out a roar that almost sounded like approval.

Luciano turned and gave Laurel a pat on the shoulder. "Shall we be off?"

The caravan was ready for the prince's morning greeting. His knights, soldiers, advisors, handlers, and the few guides accompanying them were lined up along the carriages and carts. They stood at attention, having finished preparing the wagons earlier. I stood among the guides, as was my place.

Laurel stepped to the front of the caravan with Luciano following. "I present to you, Prince Luciano di Aldebrandi, keeper of..."

And like every day, Luciano cut him off. "No need for formalities, Knight Laurel. These are my men. I know them and they me." These men had been traveling with the prince for more than two years, and Laurel's insistence on the royal introduction had become a bit of a joke. They placed bets on how long Luciano would listen before he ended it.

The caravan set off and I rode in the back. I enjoyed the prince's company, but the closer we got to the merchants, the more the whole farce weighed on me. When I looked him in the eye, all I saw was a dead man. I stayed away as much as possible.

But Laurel rode up on his black Andalusian, eyeballing me the entire time. "The prince demands your presence, traveling woman."

"I am at his at Lordship's service." I gave the horse a kick and Laurel and I rode in step towards the front of the caravan. The caravan spanned nearly a mile riding single file. It took almost half an hour to go the distance, and Laurel glared at me the entire time. "Speak your piece, Knight Laurel."

The old man grunted and spat. "His Lordship is more trusting of you foreign dogs, but you'll not fool me. It's his coffers you serve."

"You don't know that half," I whispered to myself in response.

For a time, I thought Laurel hated me because of my black robes or because I covered my hair and face. I thought it could have been because my skin was darker than what he was accustomed to, but he treated the other guides with the utmost respect. Eventually, though, I decided that Laurel was just more perceptive than most and he knew best when someone meant his prince harm. He was a ferocious warrior, but it was his ability to spot a liar that made him such a valuable guard.

I pulled up alongside Luciano and Laurel kept back, riding close enough to intervene while still being respectful.

"My dear lady." The prince bowed in his saddle. "The van treats you well, I hope."

"As always, Your Highness."

"The tales the guides tell of these Shadow Merchants are quite fantastic."

"What have you heard, Your Highness?"

"When I left court, it was on a rumor of their...what was it called? Bazaar of the Mists, I believe. My father called me a fool." He grew quiet. He always did at the mention of his father.

There were primary sources--journals and such--that showed King Aldebrandi had begged Luciano not to go. He warned him if he traveled so far beyond the borders of Domini, he could do nothing to save him.

"He said I would surely die."

He was right. It almost slipped from my mouth. I bit my tongue and looked away, unable to look him in the eye. I could tell by Laurel's glare he knew I'd held something back. "You will return with treasures that will raise your kingdom to new heights, Your Highness." What a lovely lie.

"What sort of magic do they offer?"

"I cannot say what awaits you. The Shadow Merchants' wares are everchanging. Shifting like the desert sands, as they say."

"But what of past trips? You've seen the merchants before."

I laughed and smiled at him. "You know the merchants' wares are a tightly guarded secret, Your Highness. I am their guide. I lead those worthy to them." He tried to pry secrets out of me every day. I never budged, but he wouldn't give up. "But I can assure you that you have never encountered such marvels in all your days."

"Nonsense." The prince and I both looked back to find Laurel scowling at me like I was a thief. He blushed at having interrupted the prince but spoke up again because at this point he couldn't back down. "His Lordship's collection of rarities and antiquities is unrivaled. You insult him by saying otherwise."

"Knight Laurel, you will not speak to our dear traveler in such tones. Interrupt again and..."

Just then, my pendant loosed a pale blue beam of light that pierced the horizon like a superheated arc laser. It was the signal I'd been waiting days for. I'd been using the pendant as a transponder to keep us heading in the right direction, and this meant preparations were complete. It usually just emitted an occasional burst of light to keep us on track, but this time it was a steady beam that signaled it was time to get things underway.

The beam rattled my chest and took my breath away. I nearly fell off the horse, but the prince rode up beside me and caught me. I just wish I'd had some warning before they activated it.

"My word, that never ceases to put a start in me." The prince helped me back into my saddle.

"My apologies, Your Highness. The Shadow Merchants' magics are sudden and...unpredictable."

"It seems a different breed this time." He was smiling. He could sense an end to a long and tiresome journey, and the excitement was palpable.

"Yes, your Highness. We near the end of our journey. This requires a slight course correction."

"Laurel?"

"Yes, Your Highness?" Laurel rode off along the caravan shouting orders to the prince's men. "Caravan left! Due nor'easterly!"

The caravan took up the call. "Caravan left! Due nor'easterly!"

The prince and I rode side by side, leading the caravan along the path of the beam. Now that we were alone, he asked, "My lady, I am curious. Why is it you refuse to share your name? It breeds great distrust in Knight Laurel."

I wanted to say, *he's right not to trust me*, but instead I told him, "I have no name."

"You jest."

"I am a servant of the Shadow Merchants. My name is my duty, and therefore, I am the Traveler. Nothing more."

"My dear Traveler, have you no place to lay your head?" The look of sadness on Luciano's face spoke volumes about his character. I'd never known the rich and powerful to be compassionate, but I suppose there were good people in all tax brackets.

"The world is my pillow; the road my home. And besides, Your Highness, home is not where you lay your head, but who accompanies you on your journey."

We rode in silence for a while. He seemed to be contemplating the idea of not having a home. He was like that, drifting off into thought for long stretches. I'd often find him riding far ahead of the caravan or staring up at the stars. I wondered what he made of it, the idea of a life on the road. He seemed to enjoy the adventure, but I could tell he missed home.

We rode for hours. The sun was going down over the horizon, and he said, "I often feel that I am not at home when I'm at home." I let the comment settle in the space between us. How was it possible that we could have so much in common? Humanity had changed so much from his time to mine, but at its core, we were still the same.

He rarely spoke about his family, and when he did, it was guarded. I'd read through his files, so I knew a bit of what he went through. First, he'd shunned the priesthood, which had enraged his father and isolated him from his siblings. Then, he endorsed a petition to create a farmers' council. His mother had always stood by his side, but it wasn't enough to keep him from choosing the road. My guess was that this whole trip was to get back in good graces with his family.

"I think," he said, staring off over the dunes, "that a life of traveling would not be such an ill fate."

"It is a blessing and a curse." I told him the truth whenever I could.

The sun lowered over the hills and the sky glowed violet. My pendant shimmered and the Shadow Merchants made their entrance. They always did have a flare for theatrics.

The horizon rippled not unlike the waves of heat that made the air shimmer, but the ripples grew and shook the sands up off the ground. The Earth trembled, and the royal handlers had to calm the horses as the tremors grew.

"My lady..." The prince held my hand to brace himself at the pure astonishment.

The sands rose in dancing streams; ebbing, shifting, and arcing about in all directions. They formed a base and solidified into rock and steadily began layering and layering until the stream of sand took the shape of an old desert castle. I'd helped design this gaudy thing. The domed turrets and tiled mosaics were my ideas. They were a bit archetypal–and frankly not my best work–but the prince had never seen anything like them, so to him, they would have seemed magical even if they hadn't materialized from the sand.

Laurel rode up beside the prince and stared in awe.

"Wicked sorcery," he said.

"Wondrous magic," the prince said.

"The Shadow Merchants," I said.

I led Luciano and Laurel to the main gate and it rose as we approached. The sands swirled up again like when the castle formed, but this time, much smaller. They coalesced into the shape of a man, and suddenly, the captain stood before us. He wore silk teal robes, smoked a pipe that curved from his mouth, and wore a wide-brimmed, pointed hat that I suppose he thought made him look like a wizard.

Laurel moved to draw his sword, but the prince stopped him.

I made the introduction. "Your Highness, I present to you the Lord Ambassador of the Shadow Merchants."

The captain stroked the bushy beard he'd grown for this assignment and bowed to the prince with a little flip of his hat. "Come, fair prince," he said as he turned and headed towards the castle. "You've traveled far for our wares. Let's not tarry."

He made his way inside, but the prince hesitated. "Our journey has come to a close, Your Highness," I said. I ushered him in, bowing as I led him to the entrance. "Now we barter."

The inner décor was a mix of the captain's theatrics and the blue light from the holo-emitters. We masked them as sconces with an ethereal blue flame. The glow they cast made the stones shimmer like coral. The walls were inlaid with mosaics of marble tile placed to reflect the light and create a dazzling shimmer.

We'd played this con before, and it always did wonders leading the mark down a series of gaudy halls and stairwells. We went down a spiral staircase that was dark and ominous. The lights dimmed as we descended, and for a long while, the bottom was not visible. *Wonder with just a hint of fear,* as the captain liked to say.

At the bottom of the stairwell, we came to the antechamber of the merchant's bazaar. They'd gone with a portal layout that the captain thought up. The walls were covered with velvet curtains in various shades of maroon, orange, and gold. Behind the curtains were swirling portals of the same shimmering blue light as the sconces.

"With so many shops at hand, it's always a difficult choice," the captain said. "I can provide recommendations if you like."

The captain led us down a hallway of portals. The prince gawked in awe. Not all of them were active, but he didn't need to know that. Laurel stood in between Luciano and the captain, ready to lash out at the slightest sign of trouble.

"Have you a preference, fair prince? The finest silks? Exotic spices to ignite the palette? A trove of tomes and scrolls? What's your fancy, sire?" The captain looked over his shoulder and winked at the prince. "Maybe a comely lass to warm your bed?"

Luciano blushed in the most adorable way. "I... no... that... no, thank you."

This was the right moment to capitalize on Luciano's modesty. I gently rested my hand on his and his cheeks turned redder than molten metal. "Shall we let the Ambassador lead us?"

"Yes..." He cupped my hand in his and bowed slightly; almost a curtsy, really. "Yes, that will do."

"In that case, arms and armaments for a royal army."

"There is no need," Laurel said, sneering at the captain. "We carry the finest swords of the king's forge."

"Mind your place, Laurel." Luciano gave the captain a pat on the shoulder and smiled. "Lead on, Ambassador."

At the end of the hall, the captain stopped at one of the portals. Without a word, he stepped through. The prince and Laurel shared a shocked glance as the captain seemed to have disappeared into thin air. It was nothing but a simple light trick, but it was convincing.

Laurel stepped in front of the prince, barring his path. "Allow me, your Highness. We know not if these magics are safe. He stepped through, and then a few moments later he peeked his head through the veil. "This worried me, your Highness, but it appears safe. It leads to a distant land."

The prince and I stepped through and we were in the feudal Japanese deck. This one was Kajiya's. He said it helped him get in touch with his roots, and to his credit, it was impeccably designed. We were at a hot spring in a snow-capped mountain. The glint of the sun on the snow was a nice touch, but the crisp wind was what really sold it. There was a lone Edo era inn that Kajiya had built to exacting detail, replete with the typical curved pagoda-style roof and paper doors and windows.

When we entered, the captain instructed us to remove our boots. Laurel griped about it, but Luciano shut him down. A maid, which I could only guess was one of Kajiya's bots, led us down a series of hallways that opened into a cavernous armory. The ceiling was two stories high, and the walls displayed swords and spears. Kajiya sat cross-legged on a cushion at the end of the room flanked by life-size wooden dummies in full suits of samurai armor. At his feet were a dozen or so small spheres of what looked like crystalized amber.

Kajiya bowed deeply as the prince approached, crossing his fingers and pressing his forehead to the tatami mats.

"Fair prince, may I introduce Master Kajiya, the smith of the merchants."

"You honor us," Kajiya said, keeping his bow.

"Please rise, dear smith." Luciano was never one for formalities.

Kajiya sat up but kept his posture rigid and his hands cupped in his lap. "I see your knight has found my blades."

Luciano turned and founding Laurel inspecting a katana with the eye of an expert. "What have you found, Laurel?".

He turned at the mention of his name. "Fine blades, but hardly worth the trip."

"There is nothing sharper." Kajiya's flat matter-of-factness was more of a boast than any boast could have been. Laurel took the bait.

"A merchant's bravado."

"Test your blade on my armor."

"Excuse me?"

Kajiya gestured towards one of the dummies. "Test your blade."

Laurel looked to Luciano for direction and Luciano nodded. Laurel approached the dummy, unsheathing his sword. He took a wide stance and held the sword with both hands. He lifted the sword over his head and swung down like he was chopping wood with an axe. He cut through the armor at the shoulder and dug deep into the dummy. I couldn't help but gasp. I hadn't expected the old man to be so strong. If that was a person, it would have been certain death.

Kajiya, however, did not seem impressed. "Test my blade," he said, gesturing towards the other dummy.

Laurel sheathed his blade and approached the wall of swords. "Which one, merchant?"

"Any. They are all of equal quality."

Laurel grabbed one at random and made his way to the other dummy. He took the same stance and used the same technique, but this time, his swing cut straight through the dummy, slicing it clean in half.

Luciano smiled. "Load my caravan with a complement of these blades."

"As you say, fair prince." The captain waved at the bot and it ran off like a good servant. "Shall we move on?"

"Not just yet." Luciano pointed at the amber spheres at Kajiya's feet. "What of these...baubles? What are they?"

"I call them sun stones," Kajiya said. "They are of my own design." He stood and picked one up. "If you will follow."

We stepped outside, and before anyone could speak, Kajiya whipped the stone at the side of the mountain. It hit and erupted into a sphere of white hot light. It burned for a moment or two and blinked away as fast as it had appeared. The side of the mountain had a new concave crater.

The prince and his knight were too stunned to speak. I took the moment to sidle up to the captain. "We're giving them plasma grenades?" I whispered.

"Relax. We're monitoring the timeline. It's all going according to plan."

"I'll take all of them," the prince said.

We made our way through several other portals. Each of the crew had their own little flairs. Rajneet sold a powder that burned through metal. Hamlin was dressed like a horror movie vampire; he sold an invisibility cloak. Adalé wore a robe like mine, but hers was gold and she wore elaborate jewelry, always trying to one-up me. She sold him a shield made of mist.

Laurel warned the prince against trusting the reliability of the "magics" we sold, and I nearly cried. I wanted to speak up and tell the prince to turn back, to run home to his father, to accept his life as a priest, to give up his silly schemes for validation. But what would it matter? If the prince left now with nothing, he'd still die out in the desert.

I stepped away for a moment while the prince gawked at a cream that could knit wounds. I needed a minute to myself to catch my breath, but the captain followed me.

"You all right?"

"No." I dropped the hood and rubbed my hands through my hair, massaging the throbbing vein in my scalp. "This is wrong."

"You get too attached to these people. He died more than a thousand years ago."

"He's right there. He's alive right now!"

"Right now is relative."

"I..."

"This isn't going to affect the mission, is it?" He was staring me down. He wouldn't drop it. No way of getting around it.

"No. It won't affect the fucking mission. Even if I tried to save him, he'd still end up dead."

"And don't forget it." He patted me on the back like I was a child. "You can retire after this one."

He stepped back through the portal and I had to use every ounce of restraint in my very being to resist the urge to scream.

The prince and the captain stepped back into the hall. Luciano looked ecstatic. The "treasures" we were peddling were beyond his wildest dreams. He saw me leaning against the wall and his smile faded.

"Are you unwell, dear Traveler? You look ill. Shall I call the van's healer?"

I realized that I'd been crying. I hadn't even noticed the tears on my cheeks and it was too late to hide them. The captain glared at me, and Laurel was clearly suspicious. I had to say something. I had to think fast.

"Our journey draws to a close. I fear I'll never see you again." I hadn't expected to say that, even as the words spilled from my mouth. The anger and suspicion from the captain and Laurel only grew, but Luciano smiled in a way I'd never seen before. He had such a genuine tenderness about him. Maybe in a different life, he could have been a poet or an artist. He didn't have to say it, but I knew then that he loved me.

"Shall we continue, fair prince?" The captain tried to urge Luciano on to the next set of trinkets, but he wouldn't take his eyes off me. He held my hands in his and I couldn't hold back my tears.

"Yes," the prince finally said.

"I've saved something special for last," the captain said.

"Indeed." Luciano squeezed my hand. I didn't want him to let go.

"On to the next wonder, then," the captain said.

He leaned in to whisper in my ear. "We'll speak later."

They went ahead, and for a moment, I couldn't bring myself to follow. I wanted that moment to last forever. I savored it for as long as I could. Eventually though, I lifted my robes and ran to catch up.

"This is marvelous," the prince said as we made our way into the next illusion.

We were in the captain's "zoo," a lush approximation of the Serengeti under a rose-tinted sky. The captain had put a lot of work into this program; he knew it would be the tipping point for the prince. He modeled it after the Acidalia City Zoo on Mars. I'd been there when I was a girl, and I remembered the red walkways of cobbled stone and brick. He captured the amber woodgrain barricades on the exhibits and the autumn foliage on the red oaks. Martians always did have an affinity for the color red, and the captain was a proud son of the red planet.

Most of the animals on display were holographic overlays; simple light tricks, really. The tigers, lions, elephants, and even the sharks were all just elaborate programs that played on a loop. There were a few of Kajiya's bots, though. The giraffe was particularly authentic with its long, loping gait and algorithms that kept it munching on leaves. For the most part, though, the whole thing was nothing but refracted holograms.

The sounds in the zoo were too real for my liking, though. I knew it was fake, but I still found it unsettling. I rarely stepped foot inside while the program was running. The lions' roars echoed through the hall, reverberating through each of the distinct habitats. There were chirping birds and grunting beasts, but despite knowing exactly where the speakers were hidden, it made my skin crawl. I could only imagine how the prince felt.

"I've never seen something so wondrous in all my days," he said. And of course, I knew it was the truth. "Are all these beasts for sale?"

"Some, fair prince, but I have something exquisite for you."

At the back of the zoo was an exhibit guarded by a holographic dome. The dome was meant to mimic a ship's shield array, but really it was just for show. The captain told the prince it was one of his "magics."

Beyond the shield was a tropical rainforest. Of course, in reality, it was a cell barely larger than the prince's traveling tent, but what we saw was a dense wall of palm trees and thick vines tinted red under the sunset. The forest was dark under the canopy of trees, and the deep, raspy growls that emanated from within sent shivers down my spine.

The captain pulled a bamboo whistle from his robe and blew three sharp notes. In response came a series of vicious shrieks. The trees rustled as the beasts drew closer. The prince and his knight took a step back as the shrieks grew louder. I hated these things.

Three raptors charged out from the forest, snarling and hissing as they approached. The captain blew the whistle and they were silent. Laurel had drawn his sword, and honestly, I couldn't blame him. Kajiya was so proud of these things. He took a sick pleasure in seeing the fear they instilled in people. They were behind the forcefield, but frightening, nonetheless.

"These are..." the prince hesitated. He was afraid and fascinated all at once. "...terrible lizards. Are they dragons?"

"No, fair prince. These predate dragons. They are old beasts, and the last of their line. There are no others in all the kingdoms."

"Your Highness, the beasts look wild." Laurel had his sword and shield at the ready. "They'll surely do more harm than good in battle."

"Quite the contrary, dear knight." The captain waved his hand and some ancient glyph he'd found in the ship's lexicon appeared across the forcefield. It was a fancy little trick. Then, with a puff of smoke, the shield was gone. The lizards stepped out from their exhibit onto the cobblestones and everyone except the captain stepped back.

"Are you mad?" Laurel took up a battle stance. He'd be no match against three of Kajiya's bots, but he was stalwart in protecting his prince.

At this point, the prince was terrified. He had unsheathed his sword, but even though he was well-trained, his hand quivered at the sight of them. The raptors stood still, making no further moves towards us. I rested my hand atop the prince's and nodded. He hesitated for a moment and sheathed his blade.

"No, fair knight; for you see, in addition to my duties as ambassador," he blew his whistle in one long raspy note, "I am also a gifted beast mage."

In unison, the raptors bowed to the prince like a trio of proper gentlemen. Luciano's face lit up in delight. Of all the wonders he'd seen that day, this was surely the greatest in his eyes.

"I'll take all three."

✳ ✳ ✳

I waited for the prince in his tent. There was the matter of sorting out payment for all the "treasures" he'd procured. At that moment, the prince presented the Shadow Merchants with chests full of diamonds and gold. The captain would feign his approval at the sight of the rare gems, but it was the simple things that carried the highest value. Along with the jewels, there were silks and clothing, tapestries from Luciano's kingdom, arms and armor from his forge, and several of personal trinkets from the prince himself. These would be timestamped and verified once onboard the ship.

Anything from the lost prince would fetch a fortune. He always died, and his caravan was always lost. Whether it was in the desert, at sea, or scattered across the land by bandits, next to nothing of Luciano's expedition ever survived. We would have the greatest haul of his personal belongings ever collected, and it was sure to make all of us very wealthy. The closer we got to our prize, though, the less I wanted it.

I stepped out from the tent and watched as the treasures were exchanged. Kajiya and the crew loaded them onto bots that resembled elephants. A procession of them entered the old palace that was our ship in disguise. It took nearly an hour to load everything into the cargo bay and prep the ship.

When the line of carts and elephants finally stopped and the transaction came to a close, the captain retreated into the ship and the cloak went up. The effect was a reversal of their elaborate entrance. The sands swirled away in long tendrils, returning to the dunes, and leaving the prince and his caravan alone under the desert sky.

The prince approached the tent with a broad smile. He was satisfied with himself, surely. If I hadn't known him so well I might have mistaken it for smugness. He'd set out on a journey to bring the greatest treasures in the world to his kingdom, but what he was really after was a definition of himself that was his own, rather than one prescribed to him by birth. The fact that he thought he'd succeeded broke my heart.

"Tell me true, Your Highness, were you pleased with the Shadow Merchants?"

He removed his cloak and tossed it across his bed. I'm sure there was some formality that should have been followed, but Luciano was his own man, now more than ever.

He plopped down in his velvet lined chair and stuffed a handful of grapes in his mouth. "Unparalleled, lady Traveler. I've never been so happy in all my life. I expected greatness, but there are not words for the marvels of the merchants."

He seemed to realize he was ignoring his royal decorum. On his table was a celebratory feast of roast duck, candied squash, trays of cured meats, and an assortment of fresh fruits and vegetables. He stood and ushered me to sit.

"But look at me, where are my manners? Sit, lady Traveler. There's a feast, courtesy of your merchants."

"I'm afraid I must decline."

"But why? This is a night of celebration."

I wanted to tell him. For a moment, I wondered what would become of us if I ran off with him. We'd never run a simulation for that. Maybe he would have lived. Maybe I could have saved him. Surely, the captain would hunt me down and it would all be for nothing, but there were so many possibilities in the multiverse.

I thought about it. I really did. Luciano stared at me as I contemplated. He always died, I had to remind myself. He always died.

"I'm a wanderer, Your Highness."

"Luciano. Please, call me Luciano." He placed his hands on my shoulders and without thinking, I wrapped my hands in his. "I am the fifth son. I have no claim to the throne, nor any desire for it. I can marry as I see fit, and with the riches of your merchants, I can choose my own path."

"It is my fate to wander."

He tried to lower my hood, to catch a closer glimpse of my face, but I wasn't ready for him to see me. I pulled away, crying. He saw the tears in my eyes and said, "My lady?"

A scream rang out through the caravan and the prince turned to see where it had come from. I activated the cloak hidden in my necklace, and when he turned back, I'd vanished.

He ran from the tent, screaming for me. "My lady. Dear Traveler. Don't go."

Laurel approached in full armor. He carried his sword and shield rather than one of the katanas from Kajiya. He was smart not to trust them.

"Knight Laurel, where is our Lady Traveler? Have you seen her?"

"This is not the time, Your Highness." Laurel pointed towards the cages with his sword. The beast master and all the prince's animals were dead. They were gutted by Kajiya's bots. The doors of the raptor's cages were ripped clean off and thrown several yards. Their shrieks and roars echoed from all directions, and the wind had picked up, spinning the sand into great swirls that obscured everything in sight.

"Hear me, Laurel; you will find our Lady Traveler. If there is danger afoot, you will protect her."

"Your men are our priority. I beg you. They have served well."

"Find her, Laurel." His voice was a low growl and there was a fire in his eyes like I'd never seen before.

"I swore an oath to my king to protect you and this van, not that foreign witch. She has clouded your mind. I do this with great regret, my prince."

Laurel was off running towards the worst of the raptor's roars. I followed. The captain wanted me there to monitor the violence. I was to ensure the deed was done properly.

The prince's men were massacred. They fought with the swords that Kajiya had supplied and the blades shattered with each blow they landed on the lizards. Many of them died scrambling to unsheathe their own swords. The rest died fiddling with the junk we'd sold them. They tried to slip on their invisibility cloaks, only to find they were nothing but blankets. The shield of mist vanished into smoke and the powder that melted metal was nothing but dust. It was an ugly slaughter.

A few of the prince's men escaped, but that was part of the plan. Their survival allowed the story of the prince's death to spread. History would remember it as Luciano dying at the hands of wild beasts. The story would grow in grandeur, retold with dragons or some other mythical creatures, and subside to something mundane like jackals or wolves, only to swell again. Like all mysteries, it would ebb and flow and change with the ages, truth mixing with fiction. Luciano and the van would be lost to the annals of time. Temporal scans of the era would show nothing out of the ordinary.

The raptors pressed the surviving soldiers in towards the prince's tent. They fought valiantly, but the bots' teeth were made from the same blend of metals and alloys used to build temporal frigates. More and more of the men fell.

Laurel, though, fought like a monster. The raptors were too fast for him to land a blow, but he kept them at bay with his lunging strikes and shield thrusts. The bots' algorithms kept them from pressing too hard against the old knight, because he might actually do some damage with his sword.

I let the battle continue until Laurel was the only one left. He retreated to the prince's tent. I called off the raptors and decided I would finish this on my own.

Laurel stood at the entrance to the prince's tent, urging him to leave.

"We mustn't tarry, Your Highness. We leave now, or we die."

"She left us behind..." I could hear the tears in his voice. He was heartbroken. I had to make it quick before I lost my nerve.

"She gone. She's not coming--"

I used one of Kajiya's plasma grenades to kill Laurel. Best to have it done quickly. There was nothing left of him but a seared patch of glass where the sand had been superheated. Luciano came running. The glass crunched under his feet and he lifted up a handful of sand where Laurel had just been.

I removed my robes and decloaked. I wanted Luciano to see me for what I was. He looked up and saw me standing there in a temporal induction suit. The fine white sheen of the suit and the glow of the holographic overlays must have made me appear to be some sort of witch or a goddess in his eyes, but it was my face that caught his eye.

"You're beautiful," he said. He approached with his hand outstretched, not the least bit afraid of me or the raptors at my sides. "You could have been royalty."

I raised my gun, hand trembling, palm sweaty, heart racing. "You always died. Nothing could have changed that."

One clean shot to his chest put him down. He toppled to his knees and there was a hole where his heart had been.

I let out a gasp I hadn't known was there, trapped in the back of my throat

"Is it done?" the captain's voice said over the comm.

"It's done."

Wind swept over the sands as the Solar Shadow decloaked. The faint hum of its engines told me we were ready to depart. Our hold was full with a bounty fit for the grandest of historical collectors. The crew would be celebrating.

The rear bay door opened, and the pale blue of the ship's light poured out. The captain was waiting for me.

"Time to go."

I took one last look at Luciano slumped down in the sand with his heart burned away. Tears welled up and I knew I couldn't stay long before the emotion overwhelmed me.

"You always died."

Or at least that's what I tell myself.

When You Get to Heaven

Father Benedetto relished his time in the confessional. Nothing in his schedule quite compared. Not sermons, not social work, not even the occasional wedding. All the priests in his parish had their skills; his was digging deep into the psyches of his parishioners and rooting out their inner demons. There was such a deep level of trust that came of it, a threefold connection between him, his parishioner, and God. He often thought that if not for the priesthood, he likely would have wound up in psychiatry.

Lately, though, the confessional had lost its appeal. So few came to confess their sins, and Father Benedetto spent most of his time twiddling his thumbs and counting the beads of his rosary. But there was more than that. The cramps were what really spoiled it for him. In the past few weeks, it seemed that every time he stepped into the booth his stomach protested, and the taste of bile rose in his throat. He tried his best to control it, but it only grew worse and worse. All the antacids in the world seemed powerless against it. The only real cure he'd found was to step out of the booth and catch his breath.

One dreary weekday afternoon he did just that. The cramps hit suddenly and bowled him over, leaving him gasping for air. It was the most powerful attack yet, and he nearly took the door off its hinges as he fell from the booth. He leaned against a nearby pillar, taking long, slow breaths as the pain eased away.

A woman called his name. "Father Benedetto? Excuse me, can I have a moment of your time?"

A young mother and her daughter sat in the back pew. Morning mass had ended hours earlier, but all were welcome in the church. "I hate to trouble you, Father, but could you spare a moment for my daughter?"

Father Benedetto's legs were shaking, but he pressed a crease from his robe, stood up straight, and made his way to sit next to the girl. She couldn't have been more than five.

"How may I be of service, young lady?"

"Do you..." She blushed and looked down at her shoes. Her long black bangs fell over her face, barely hiding her sheepish smile.

"Don't be shy, dear."

She kept her eyes on her shoes. "Do you know what heaven is like?"

Benedetto stroked his beard and gave the question a bit of thought. Clearly, the girl had been pondering it for a while. "Well, I haven't been yet, but I imagine that heaven is like being enveloped in God's love. Do you know what it means to be content?"

The girl nodded. Still, she would not look at Benedetto.

"I think that heaven is contentment." He tussled her hair and smiled at her. "Does that answer your question?"

"Father Benedetto," the girl said, "when you get to heaven, tell God you need his help."

"I...need his help?"

She tipped her face up to him and her eyes glowed white hot. No pupil, no iris; just a blazing white like staring into the sun. He wasn't sure if they were the eyes of God or something more sinister.

"Father, when you get to heaven--"

"Enough!" the mother screamed.

She grabbed the girl by the wrist and yanked her out of the pew. The girl blinked, and her eyes returned to normal. "We've taken enough of the Father's time." The mother dragged her daughter off towards the exit. Father Benedetto watched in awe and terror as they left.

He sat in the pew for what seemed like ages. Never in all his life had he experienced such a brush with the divine. Since arriving at St. Peter's Church, his fellow priests had started calling him Father Secular, a nickname he embraced. He was proud to be thought of as rational and pragmatic. His faith was complex and nuanced; he thought of heaven as a state of being attainable on Earth, if only humanity were capable of it. To Father Benedetto, God was a source of morality. Whether a person believed in the deity or not, those who worked towards goodness held God in their hearts. But for the first time in years, he seriously considered the idea of a bearded man in the clouds and a red devil with a pitchfork.

When he finally stood, he found his legs were still trembling and the cramps had come on even stronger than before. It was the first time it had happened outside the confessional.

"Father?"

He looked around and saw no one.

"Father?"

It seemed to be coming from the confessional. He hobbled over to the booth on shaking legs and fell into his seat. "How may I be of service," he said, but there was no one there.

"What the hell is going on?" He rubbed the bridge of his nose and sat in silence. Was this God's work? The Devil? Or was he losing his mind? All seemed far too plausible.

"Father?"

He looked through the partition and saw wisps of smoke ebbing and flowing. He should have run, because surely there was a fire, but the smoke had form and shape. It coalesced into something resembling a man; a featureless shadow of a man, but a man nonetheless.

"Are you testing me?" he said. Whether this question was addressed to God, he couldn't tell.

"When you get to heaven," the shadow man said, "tell God you deserved better."

He stumbled out of the confessional and made a move towards the adjacent booth as thick black smoke billowed from the door. He tripped and fell on his behind as he backed away. Once he was back on his feet, he made a run for the exit on quivering legs.

He leaned against the heavy doors of the church, taking in the fresh air. It did little to ease his pain. The cramps had brought on sweat, and the sweat grew to a fever. It was as if the pain in his stomach had spread like a disease, infecting every inch of him. He thought he might pass out from it.

Downtown Chicago on a weekday. The streets were full of business people and tourists. None of them seemed to pay any attention to the priest gasping and wheezing on the steps of the church. A chubby woman with a fanny pack looked him dead in the eye and said, "When you get to heaven, tell God it didn't have to be this way."

She walked off as if nothing had happened and disappeared into the crowd. He followed her for about half a block, but then he saw something climbing up out of the river. It looked like smoke, and at first, he thought there was a fire, but it seemed to be moving towards him. It was a thick black fog pouring up out of the water and swallowing everything in its wake. Dark shadows whipped and writhed like the tentacles of a kraken.

But what was even more frightening than the fog was that no one else to seemed to notice. These people were milling about their day, unaware of the monstrous black cloud devouring the streets of Chicago. Couldn't they see they were all doomed?

Father Benedetto felt the urge to run so powerfully it bordered on hysteria, but his legs refused to move. He watched the writhing smoke tunnel through the downtown skyscrapers. It moved with purpose, billowing towards him. Everything it touched was swallowed in pure darkness. It was certain death, he knew it in his bones, but he could not move a muscle.

A business man in a crisp suit bumped into Benedetto and said, "When you get to heaven, tell God the deck was stacked against you."

When he looked back, the shadows were nearly upon him. Benedetto took off at a full sprint in the other direction. His body was sore, his nerves were shot, and his sanity was failing, but fear and adrenaline pushed him forward. He had no idea where he was going or what he would do when he got there, but he ran.

He came to an intersection, and from the south and east, the foggy shadows gushed through the streets like whitewater rapids. It was as if they funneled him towards something, but what choice did he have? There was only one direction available to him.

He ran down State Street, dipping and dodging through department store shoppers and businesspeople. He hopped over beggars and leapt over cars as they honked at the crazy man dashing out into busy crossings. The shadows were gaining on him, and not a soul but himself seemed even remotely concerned.

Then he saw it. Holy Name Cathedral. He'd been by countless times, but he'd yet to step inside. On his nightly walks he found himself drawn here, and he would stop and stare for long stretches, never daring to enter. It was almost his church, but when he saw it for the first time he felt a shudder in his gut and he begged for a different parish.

And now that he was standing here, he couldn't recall what had drawn him to Chicago in the first place. His earliest memories were all from his mother's home in Connecticut. As far as he could remember, he had lived there his whole life. But Holy Name was familiar the moment he saw it. He'd never been there though, he was sure of that. In fact, before joining St. Peter's, he'd never even been to Chicago. So why couldn't he shake that terrible sense of déjà vu?

The shadows had faded, and the city was itself again, as though nothing had happened. There was no sign that anything had happened at all; not on the buildings or in the streets, and certainly not on the faces of the blissfully unaware pedestrians. He was losing his mind, he'd never been more certain. He wanted to turn back, to turn tail and run home, to curl up in a ball and pretend this nightmare wasn't real.

But the church called to him. The feeling that he'd been there before was magnetic. He couldn't turn away. He heard a whisper in his ear, "When you get to heaven, tell God you deserve forgiveness." He turned and saw no one nearby. Who said that? Was it the woman in the leather jacket? The man with the stroller? Everything seemed a blur. The world faded away and there was only the church.

He made his way across the street and the smoke rose up all around the church, forming an impenetrable wall. This shadowy beast would not let him retreat. There was no exit past this point and he pressed on. As he approached the heavy double doors, the smoke slithered its way past him and threw itself into a barricade. In its own hideous way, it was fascinating. It took on a liquid sheen, thick, black, and viscous. The way it Upwaters. It entranced him, and he could not look away. Tendrils of smoke leapt out only to disappear again under the tide.

It made no move toward him. It seemed clear in his mind that the only way forward was straight through it. He took a deep breath, working up his courage, and reached his hand into the fog. A tingle ran up his arm and became a vibration. He couldn't see his arm through the blackness of the shadow and he pawed aimlessly in search of the door handle, but it was as if there was no door at all. The vibration grew into heat, and the heat into burning. Before long, his arm was an ember. Fissures of molten heat cracked open, and his skin flaked away like a sheet of paper put to flame.

A voice rumbled in his head, "When you get to heaven--"

He screamed in agony, trying to wrestle himself free, but the tendrils caught hold of him, yanking him back in a game of tug of war that he couldn't hope to win. They burned away his flesh until it was nothing but dry bone.

"--tell God you won't take any more of his shit."

The shadows released him and he tumbled backwards, falling hard to the ground. He reached frantically to his arm and found it unharmed.

The voice echoed in his head. "When you get to heaven...when you get to heaven...when you get to heaven." He couldn't shake it. "When you get to heaven...when you get to heaven...when you get to heaven." He pounded his head on the steps of the church, but he couldn't quiet the voice. "When you get to heaven...when you get to heaven...when you get to heaven."

"Shut up!" he screamed at the shadows. "Shut up shut up shut up!"

He charged at the wall of shadow. The fear was gone and all that remained was the compulsive need to have the wretched voice gone. The fog swallowed him up and he ran and ran for what seemed like forever. It was acid in an open wound. His skin cracked into glowing fissures. "When you get to heaven...when you get to heaven...when you get to heaven."

And then he was through. The fog broke and faded away. He fell flat on his back and stared up at the inside of the city's most famous church. His arm was fine. No ash or embers. No burns at all.

He contemplated lying there and never getting up. Never in his life had he been so terrified and exhausted. *When you get to heaven* played on repeat, and he couldn't fathom where it had come from. Was heaven even real? He'd peered behind the veil and seen a glimpse of hell, but heaven seemed a distant impossibility at this point. Maybe if he just stayed on the ground and wept until he was dead he'd have an answer. But maybe there was nothing waiting on the other side, just darkness, and he was losing his mind.

And then he heard it again, but from somewhere inside the church. "When you get to heaven, tell God you got what was coming to you." It was a boy's voice. He didn't want to get up. He didn't want to face whatever was waiting for him. But the need to keep going was compulsive, and even though his mind and every muscle in his body protested, he stood up.

The church was empty. There were lit candles on the altar. The stained glass washed the hall in reds, oranges, and yellows, and for a moment, he was in awe of its beauty.

Then he heard the voice of the boy again, echoing off the vaulted ceiling and marble floor. "Dad, what happens when you get to heaven?" A ghostly apparition of a boy and his father made their way across the altar like pillars of smoke drifting in the wind.

Benedetto approached the altar and heard the father respond. "Not now. We're in a hurry."

He remembered this. It came back so powerfully that he felt his head throb. He'd been here with his father. He'd walked down this aisle to receive communion. He'd held his father's hand. Two pieces of himself came together and made his head swim. He nearly lost his balance. He shook his head and when he opened his eyes, the church was full of apparitions.

The din of their voices was cacophonous and filled the church in a wordless hum. Time moved at a different pace for them, and they faded in and out existence at random. One of the ghosts passed through him, unaware of his presence, and it burned like the fire from the shadows.

He made his way down the aisle, avoiding the formless phantoms. They flowed together like a hundred memories stitched at the seams. One minute, a shadow blocked his path, and the next it was gone, only to be replaced by one at his side. He spun and dodged until finally he'd reached the altar.

They disappeared all at once and he was alone except for the sound of their voices. The hum of them lingered in the empty hall, but one set of voices rose up above it.

"Sister Brooke says you get to talk to God."

"Didn't I tell you to pipe down?"

"But, Dad..."

He caught sight of the ghosts of the boy and his father near the confessional booths. The father–*his* father, he knew this to be true–leaned down and scolded the boy. "Don't make me. Not here. Not with all these people around."

Benedetto watched the tears well up in the eyes of his younger self. He was there. He remembered the anger and confusion; the

106

embarrassment and guilt. "But don't you wonder what you'd say to God if you could to talk to him?"

His father grabbed his younger self and slammed the phantom boy's head into the door of the confessional. Benedetto felt the blow on his forehead. When he touched his hand to it, it came back bloody.

"Look what you made me do." The ghosts faded away, but he could still hear the voice of his father. "When I tell you to shut your mouth, you shut your mouth."

The ghosts were gone and the door to the confessional swung open with a rusty shriek.

"Jesus Christ," Benedetto said. He'd never felt more on edge in all his life.

He stepped into the confessional and sitting on the other side of the partition was his father. It was a ghostly, ethereal version of the man, but he recognized the face. He'd died when Benedetto was a boy, but even after all these years, he still remembered the face.

"It's been four years since my last confession."

"What are you?"

"I struck my son...or...that is to say, I strike him...often."

Father Benedetto leaned in close, pressing his face against the partition. The ghost of his father did not acknowledge him. The image of the man had faded over the years; there were details he didn't immediately remember. His thick handlebar mustache was iconic, but the sagging jowls, the thick creases in his forehead, and the leathery, coarse skin were not what he pictured. It was his father, that much was clear, but in his mind, the man was much younger, more vibrant and powerful. The ghostly man beside him, despite not being entirely opaque, was very human. Nonetheless, the old emotions he stirred in Benedetto were overwhelming.

Fear and terror. That was all he'd ever felt for the man. Crippling fear that left him scared to move, scared to speak, scared to exist. No love, no joy, not even anger; just fear. It hit him like a shock from a stun gun and his muscles clenched. The pain in his stomach returned, and his jaw locked. The sight of him turned Benedetto's stomach, and the pain spread through his body.

"He acts out. He's just a kid, but I...I lose control." His father's voice quivered. "I know he hates me. I know I deserve it."

His words were shards of glass trickling down Benedetto's throat. His gut was bubbling, and he swore there was a taste of iron alongside the bile.

"He fantasizes about killing me. I know he does. He dreams about bleeding me dry." This thing that was his father stared at him with eyes that glowed white hot. "There's a darkness in you. A pit so hollow that no amount of prayer and piety can fill it. Promise me this," his father said, pressing his hand against the partition, "When you get to Heaven, tell God you did what you had to."

"Enough!" Father Benedetto screamed. He stormed out of the confessional and ripped open the door on his father's side of the booth. It was empty. "God help me."

He made the sign of the cross and took a moment to catch his breath. An old Polaroid photo lay on the bench where his father had just been sitting. The colors were faded to a fuzzy sepia, but he recognized it nonetheless. It was him and his father.

He held the photo with two fingers, like it was a dead rat. He was with his father at Sunday mass. Benedetto must have been no more than five years old and he was playing with a Matchbox car in the back pew. His father sat next to him, glaring at him with a cold contempt.

He'd forgotten. How could he have forgotten? He'd blocked so much. It was a cloudy, misshapen memory, but at the sight of that photo, it all came rushing back. The basement, the rope, the sting of his father's belt, the cursing, the kicks, the crippling sense of guilt, the pleading, the begging. His father screamed again and again, *When you get to heaven, the Lord will turn you away!* He'd beaten Benedetto's mother, too, for allowing him to bring a toy into church.

That was the last beating before his father got sick. And then it hit him. It was his fault. The guilt he'd felt when his father died. How could he ever have forgotten? His father died when he was six. *If only I hadn't been such a sinner, he wouldn't have died.* That's what he thought at the time. That's what he'd thought for years, until he buried it so deep it disappeared. He barely thought of his father after that.

109

And yet here he was, with a picture of his father, a face he hadn't seen in more than thirty years. The fear hadn't gone. He was a child again, hiding under tables, cowering in closets, trembling in his mother's arms. How had he kept it under control all these years? And how could one little picture hold so much power over him?

He hadn't seen the photo in years, not since his mother passed. He remembered finding it among her belongings, but he couldn't for the life of him recall what he'd done with it. How it had made its way here from his hometown in Connecticut was a complete mystery. Why had he kept it? How did it get here?

He flipped over the picture and saw a message written on the back. *When you get to heaven, tell God it was too late.* He sat and stared at the photo for what seemed like forever. Now that the memory was loose, he wanted nothing more than to bury it again. But once free, how could he capture this demon he'd let loose?

His foot hit something beneath the seat of the confessional. He knelt and found a simple cardboard box with the words *When you get to heaven* written all over it in red marker. Benedetto held the package to his chest, cradling it like a baby, weeping uncontrollably.

When he finally mustered the courage to open it, he found a handgun and a crucifix. He recognized these immediately as his father's. From a young age, he'd learned that there were two items he could never touch, and here they were. Beneath the gun was a note that read *When you get to heaven...*

110

And then the ghost of his father was beside him, leaning down to could whisper in Benedetto's ear. "Tell God you have no right to be there."

The cloud of fog returned, and he was surrounded by the apparitions. "You have no right," they chanted. "You have no right"

"Youhavenorightyouhavenorightyouhavenoright."

They swirled around him, forming into a black mass that enveloped him. His eyes took on the same white glow as the girl's. The fire of the shadows took over, coursing through every inch of him. He screamed in agony. A hundred voices all at once echoed in his head.

"When you get to heaven," they said.

The fog took him, and he was falling and falling and falling. He tried to resist, to escape the taunts, but they came from every direction.

"Tell God this was his fault."

"Tell God he abandoned you."

"Tell God you have no right."

"Tell God you have no right!"

"TELL GOD YOU HAVE NO RIGHT!"

He ran and ran and ran until he couldn't run anymore and finally collapsed. The shadows let go, and all the voices but one disappeared. It was his father's. "When you get to heaven, tell God you don't belong there."

And then the voices stopped. He was in a dark void, an empty blackness that stretched on forever in all directions. He shuffled forward, dragging his tired body with each step. He walked for what seemed like miles in complete silence. Not even his footfalls made a noise. It seemed to go on forever until he saw a white glow in the distance.

As he approached, the glow took on the form of a church's holy water font. He leaned against the cold marble and gazed at his reflection. His father stared back at him, and this time, when his father spoke, the words came from Benedetto's own mouth.

"When you get to heaven, tell God you have no right to be there."

The cramps that had plagued Benedetto for so many weeks came flooding back. His stomach rumbled and his muscles tensed. He emptied his gut into the holy water. The bile was thick and black, like hot globs of pitch. It darkened the water and he could no longer see his reflection.

Floating in the center of the font was a single matchbox car. The sight of it brought on a headache so ferocious that it bowled Benedetto over. He dropped to his knees, closed his eyes, and rubbed his temples until the pounding stopped. When he opened them, he found himself back inside St. Peter's Church.

When he first saw it, St. Peter's was the most beautiful place Father Benedetto had ever seen. The first time he laid eyes on it, he couldn't begin to describe the pride he'd felt at the thought of leading mass in that sacred hall. All places of worship were beautiful in their own right, but the way the light cast an orange glow over the marble at St. Peter's stirred something in his heart.

He awoke on the floor of the church, and for the first time since starting his ministry, the place was ugly to hm. He was drenched in blood, holding a pistol, and beside him were the bodies of a middle-aged man, a young mother, and her daughter. He couldn't weep for them; he had nothing left to give.

He stood up and leaned over the font to catch a glimpse of himself, but it was stained crimson with blood. His father's gun and crucifix rested on the edge of the font.

The church was darker than usual, and the only sound he could hear was the thumping of his heart. Policemen swarmed around him, and though he saw their lips moving, he heard no sound.

He raised the gun to his head as the police yelled and waved, but the world had gone silent.

"When I get to heaven," he said, "I'll tell God I'm sorry."